The Urbana Free Library

To renew materials call
217-367-4057

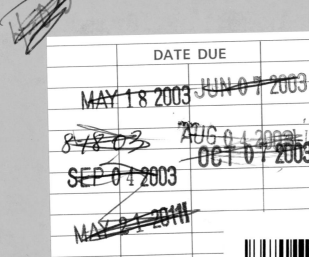

DATE DUE		
MAY 1 8 2003	JUN 0 7 2003	
8/8 03	AUG 0 4 2003	
SEP 0 4 2003	OCT 0 7 2003	
MAY 2 1 2011		

The Absolute
Perfection
of Crime

TANGUY VIEL

The Absolute Perfection of Crime

A NOVEL

Translated by Linda Coverdale

THE NEW PRESS
NEW YORK

Originally published in France as *L'absolue perfection du crime* by Les Éditions
de Minuit, 2001
Published in the United States by The New Press, New York, 2003
Distributed by W. W. Norton & Company, Inc., New York

This work has been published with the support of the French Ministry of
Culture–Centre National du Livre.

ISBN 1-56584-757-1 (hc.)
CIP data available.

The New Press was established in 1990 as a not-for-profit alternative to
the large, commercial publishing houses currently dominating the
book publishing industry. The New Press operates in the public interest rather
than for private gain, and is committed to publishing, in innovative ways,
works of educational, cultural, and community value that are often deemed
insufficiently profitable.

The New Press, 450 West 41st Street, 6th floor, New York, NY 10036
www.thenewpress.com

Printed in the United States of America

10 9 8 7 6 5 4 3 2 1

For Philippe and Laurent

The television screen above the bar, connected to an outside camera so we could see who was coming in, often out of boredom or habit I'd glance up at it, and the hair or skin color of the person ringing the bell would barely register, I'd barely notice them on the screen. But that September day, with that same television showing its single street program, in that same smoky, smelly fug, I just happened to be staring up and saw him arrive, him, Marin, three years later, the same.

It was the usual that evening, the usual hubbub, usual buzz, shadows, empty glasses. There wasn't a sudden hush, or even a dip in the volume, conversations continued, but eyes and heads twitched slightly. Low voices would talk about him at a few tables, perhaps, but they'd be whispering.

We locked eyes a moment, in freeze-frame, then embraced each other. Three years—he did say that—and you never came to see me in prison. There was a pause. It's just that guys like you, I answered, it doesn't feel right to see them in stir. We hugged again, two cognacs appeared simultaneously in front of us, we clinked glasses.

I imagined the taste of the alcohol in his mouth, the special flavor it had for him, when he still seemed to savor it even after emptying his glass, and he gestured to the barkeep, asked me with a wink if I'd have another: Always say yes, I thought—especially that evening, because you don't refuse anything to a man fresh out of prison. Several times he draped a strong arm around my shoulders, and he was smiling at me. Even if we'd tried to talk, we couldn't have, really, what with the music so loud, and me shaking inside.

Now and then Marin would put his glass on the bar and stick his cigar between his teeth. Then he'd look at me hard, and count to three with his fingers, with the thumb, index, middle finger, signing the years, insistent, three years, nodding his head in confirmation, his eyes seeming to follow the beat, three years, his eyebrows shooting up to show how long that was, as if to add to the meaning, the cumulative weight of his fingers, and he'd smile at me again, cigar clenched between his teeth, picking up his glass once more, patting me on the shoulder, then he'd tip his head back and close his eyes, drunk, tired, on edge. I could read his lips as he mouthed yet again: Three years. And he was still smiling, and I was smiling back at him, forcing my lips to stretch wide, so he wouldn't have a clue about my inner turmoil, my thoughts in a whirl, wheeling and tangling inside my skull, not a clue.

Two three more cognacs before leaving, before going outside, and I probably knew what would happen there, I'd probably dreamed it without remembering, then when we left later, it was like an iron curtain dropping from the sky, and for a few minutes I lay sprawled on the ground.

But I mean what could I have done, so I let him hit me, I went down practically at the first smack, right in the face, I couldn't do a thing, insult him maybe but I'm not crazy, I let him hit me, that's all.

The light over the entrance, the halogen that made a sort of ring in front of the club, had been switched off for some time, and Marin knelt at my side, and he whispered in my ear, he told me that he'd missed me, he kept punching me in the lungs, the belly, and that it was a shame not to visit your family now and then, twisting my arm behind my back, but that we'd forget all that like the old pals we were, slamming his elbow into my jaw, because we still had things to do together, stubbing his cigar out after that on the ground, barely an inch from my hair, then taking off, heading up the street, until he vanished in the light of dawn.

Part One

I

With everyone's headlights on because of the rain, the black Magic Marker FOR SALE sign taped to the back window became transparent, I remember, so the letters appeared in the proper order in the rearview mirror. Marin had ordered that mirror separately from the United States because he'd thought it would have etched on it, in English, "Objects in mirror are closer than they appear," and he said he liked that, that sentence etched on the glass. And even when it turned out not to be there, that sentence, it was all the same to him, in the end. So we'd barely finished with the salesman when Marin was raring to install it anyway, that mirror, wanted to install it right there in the parking lot, but I said it was stupid to waste time that morning when we had a million things to do. So he waited till the next day, Saturday, because of the weekly visit to Uncle.

To go to Uncle's, in the north, coming from Marin's place, in the south, you crossed the bridge of course, then the city of course, and after the boulevards you followed the coast. The road snaked along up on the cliffs, and there were some views that made you think of the Grande Corniche in Monaco, because of the sharp turns that overlooked the sea, and the precipice glimpsed beneath the wheels. And they'd better be a good set of wheels, I'd often thought, to handle those roads, but on that score, Marin's Mercedes drove like a dream.

So the next day he'd screwed the new rearview mirror into place, then he'd driven like that, half staring at the mirror, to go see Uncle lying in bed, his old man's weight on those wooden slats, his hands perpetually folded over his stomach. Auntie was almost as old as he was and always reading, we never knew what was inside that big book with the burgundy cover, but she never closed it except when Marin tapped her on the shoulder from behind, because of the constantly open door not being guarded, with only Auntie's shoulder blocking the way. Marin, if he hadn't held back, he'd have hauled off and whopped her one, but Auntie, she had an eye like an unblinking peephole in all those wrinkles, so he controlled himself.

That rearview mirror—forgotten in a flash when he got going talking to Uncle, to Auntie, to Andrei, to me, going on about how the "work" was coming along, as he put it, the "work," describing all he'd accomplished completely on his own, you'd have thought, as though no one in that room had ever heard of him, as though at one time he'd acted without us, without Uncle, without anyone, and had taken over direction of the operation a long time ago. In a way, I've told myself since then, in a way it was true.

We weren't actually related to Uncle at all. Even that name, *Uncle,* came from too far back for us ever to find out who'd first called him that, in the room with the single window that closed so badly and rattled, so we couldn't really tell anymore if the wind, or our voices, or rather everyone's gestures were blowing a breeze out into the neglected orchard, where only a few apples grew all by themselves.

And Marin went through the list of purchases, the items in the accounts, the full summary of what was supposed to allow the "family," Uncle said, to stay afloat. It was Marin himself who'd once flicked his fingers to put quotation marks around the family. So, the "family": that was understood, along with the feeling that within those quotation marks we were bound more tightly than if we'd imagined ourselves related by blood, because of the pride of belonging to that family, the morbid compulsion to find one's place in it, Marin most of all—in suspense, it seemed, over his possible sudden and irrational expulsion when there was no reason, never had been any reason for him to be the one to go. If there was someone who should have left all that, it was me. But I didn't do it, not that day, not the days that followed, I stayed, that's my lookout.

That's our lookout, Marin would have said. And he'd blather on, thinking he was still calming down Uncle, who would fixate on his own death the second he saw us arrive, silently begging for nothing to change after he'd gone, for us to continue, he suggested, on his ruins. And I wondered: Continue what? Then Marin would get up, walk to the window and try to close it and he'd stand there, telling the windowpanes mottled with dripping rain, with mist from his breath, how victory was so near, each person's sacrifices all the more precious, failure unthinkable, and he'd always have his arms crossed behind his back. Then Uncle would close his eyes, and keep them that way, closed, for as long as we seemed to be concerned with his dreams, with the posterity of his dreams. And Andrei and I would go outside, automatically tired, we'd head down into the garden, we'd watch Marin's dark, opaque silhouette through the window, moving his lips, and I'd imagine as well, between two trees, Uncle's closed eyes, as he sighed from contentment and the heat.

He spoke less and less, Uncle, and the last few months he barely greeted us at all. Even when Marin had rejoined us several weeks before, that blessed day for Uncle when Marin had served out his sentence, the three years he'd endured in a cell three yards square, even that longed-for day Uncle hadn't been able to rev up any emotion, any tears or trembling. He'd waited for it though, that day, and aged even faster knowing Marin was in that antiquated prison. But for him the word *emotion* had probably lost all meaning.

He does it on purpose, Marin would say in the car, he does it on purpose, not talking to us. And leaving that terrible Auntie practically on her own to welcome us, another one who didn't talk, who simply fulfilled the minimal functions of language, such as "Coffee?" or "Don't make any noise—he's asleep" or "See you next Saturday." Auntie, gloomy and dried-up and stick-like, in that shared house so much like their bodies, except it was damper than their wrinkly cheeks. Because grimness, we figured, you really can't improvise that. Abandoned long ago by spontaneity and imagination, she had a face whose slightest movement of the eyes and lips packed more power than any church sermon, and as our little group arrived every Saturday, she simply withdrew into herself.

Andrei mostly, it was Andrei who said she got on his nerves, and he declined whenever possible to attend those morose meetings, those rancid Saturdays, he said, on account of that old bag. Declined particularly since it was us going to see them, Uncle and Auntie, not them visiting one of us but us ushered into that house on the brink of dilapidation to consume sadly the same coffee without sugar, the same stale cakes, the same undistinguished port, and on top of that never for a moment forgetting that we were crooks.

Because we were crooks.

And Marin would say Uncle did it on purpose, seeming even worse off than he was, why would he, why at his great age would he take pleasure in making himself older and extradecrepit. . . .

Me, Marin, I know why, and I already knew back then, but I never told you.

And so we said nothing more about it, neither Marin nor I, in the car on the way back, nothing that would have allowed a third person to get a fix on us all and our relationships among ourselves, separately or together, each one, Uncle, Auntie, Marin, Andrei, me, keeping private the knot that tied us to that state of false meditation, where words spoken carefully, stingily, and with that tone intended to keep you waiting for their light to dawn, where those words, therefore, only hinted at the hidden mass of the iceberg.

Often, driving by the outer harbor, almost home when we

crossed the bridge, we'd start talking again. We'd chat, in our so perfectly mutual desire to break the sour silence, filling the car with everything we saw, speculating on the sailboats out on the water, we'd say, "That's Rob's boat out there yes that's Rob's boat with the gray sails only he would go out in weather like this," in that monotonous rain that always (or usually) pockmarked the sea. In a way we could breathe again, as if relieved by the prospect of arriving home, by the passage from one fiefdom to another—as if all that coastline preserving the memory of Uncle in the north and all that other one edging Marin's universe in the south were partitioned off by some meridian, a frontier we would cross on the other side of that old bridge, where we could feel free, or on our own.

So I was hardly listening to him, Marin, while he was telling Uncle about current business, the "work," he said; for our survival in that world, Uncle said. He had repeated it so often: our survival. Because we have to last a little longer, Uncle would add, have to remain loyal to the world of traitors. Of traitors, yes, Marin would insist, endlessly pacing the worn, creaking parquet and faithfully echoing the aging Uncle's increasingly colorless and meager words, of traitors, that was the word that always cropped up to express the arid and cutting souls of the men in what was called that dark and dirty milieu of the local underworld. And yet we belonged to it, this local underworld.

But us, we were different. If the day ever comes when we're like them, Marin used to say, if that day comes, I swear, just shoot me through the heart. Them, they've got no sense of family, he'd say. But how times are changing, Uncle would finally observe, a man whose life, fortune, foundation had been built on firm notions of friendship, of loyalty, and he'd point out a failing here, a betrayal there, everywhere, he said, how times are changing, he repeated, sighing ten times, a man so tired of compromising, sharing, negotiating, and he begged us not to give in, Stay on your feet, he said, till your last breath, he said.

We'd certainly picked up the habit of wild ideas and dicey jobs, after all those years of the same roads taking us to the same places, without us really knowing anymore if we could still summon up some actual enthusiasm.

And the habit of not wanting to anymore—that grew along with the "sites," the "works," the "projects" we said were suicidal, enduring more painfully each time that other habit, so closely linked, of automatically stifling our wills before him, Uncle, or before his henchman, Marin. And habit, I thought, habit sometimes collapses without any warning.

For a long time already, carrying out orders, the revolvers tucked inside our jackets, the way people greeted us in the streets, the way we'd run into trouble, it was wearing us out. Tired, that was the word, of running around at night, keeping one hand in your pocket, just in case, you never know. A time comes when you dream of something different. But if you personally don't want to wind up at the bottom of a quarry, if you yourself simply want to survive, you keep going.

2

So to have thought once again that this time was different, this time they'd give it up, to remember even saying so in front of Marin five, ten times, in that car bringing us back every week from Uncle's place, of course it was an illusion that lulled us between bends in the road. He, Marin, still acting excited about his car, eyes glued to the road, shifting through the gears, fifth, fourth to take the curves, feeling the skid and gripping the wheel, when I'd spoken of that madness of going on, Marin, that stubbornness that didn't really suit you, you shot back stupidly that it was madness all right and a good thing, too, going into third gear, hands clenched, the engine screaming again, because for a long time now, that's for sure, we'd stopped speaking the same language.

There was no entrance hall at Marin's place, visitors walked directly into the big room and tried not to scare the birds, the two tame parakeets that lived there, in the living room, and started flying around as soon as they sensed our arrival. Marin pampered them, the parakeets, and it relaxed him, he said.

But what most impressed anyone advancing among the armchairs, inside the stone walls, facing the large bay window lighting the space, what was most impressive was the view of the sea below. And Marin used to joke about it: The bay window looks out over the bay, he'd tell each new arrival, each guest who marveled at the view and sat there, fascinated. But us, we didn't say the bay, ever, we said the roadstead, because that was the right word, because around there everyone said the roadstead. In other words, not the sea so necessarily constrained, not the bridge or the view out to sea, but the compact, industrious, rusted mass of the port city in front of us, what for us would forever be the roadstead, or the background. And through the binoculars kept on a small wooden table, each in turn we'd peer into the distance, at the city, the port, and we'd believe that what we were surveying, Marin most of all, he wanted to believe that what was enlarged before our eyes, the city, the sea, belonged to us. He really had to be cracked, I would later say, if three years in prison hadn't taught him a thing.

The trees in the park had long ago grown big enough to provide the privacy he required, and they looked, the trees, like aquatic plants that had ventured out onto dry land. His blue armchairs gave the impression of a departure lounge, but in front of that window you might also have felt you were looking at an aquarium, because of that same gray city out there, three-quarters of it striped by pine branches, first the port in the foreground, then the city piling up behind it and overlooking the placid water. Like a city submerged at the bottom of the sea. One day Marin said, We're not here to admire the view. And that's what it was like, a tourist agency, the blue chairs to plan your departure and up on the wall the photo of your destination.

So we'd look away, and we knew, yes, we weren't there to

admire the view, but to focus instead on a single goal, a single date that dragged our future and our purpose in life along behind it like a tractor: the next job decided on by him, Marin, ordered by Uncle but decided on by you, Marin, and giving us all headaches.

On that truly memorable Saturday, with Uncle extricated from his ancient bathrobe, installed in the dusty rocking chair we'd all thought was kaput, his hair carefully combed for the first time in months, I knew right away something was up. Even Auntie, usually sullen and sharp and bony, whose stony face refused us the slightest tenderness, she unpursed her lips when she embraced us. I remember I had time to wonder, when I saw her smile, if he'd died, Uncle. But instead of dead he was livelier than ever.

It's not my idea, he said, it's Marin's, he said, but I like it. Marin, explain it to them. And Marin explained to us, Marin went into preaching mode and presented his idea: The casino, cleaning out the casino, I thought it over in prison, this would set us up again. Andrei and I didn't move a muscle, rooted to the waxed floor of the living room, we kept listening—Marin, Uncle, like a concert for two voices, a score the two of them had written, a single word running through our heads, *casino.* That word, just by itself it had buzzed louder than a bee in our ears, when we knew by heart everything hidden behind those six letters, *casino,* the power of money, the security muscle, and the faces of men more powerful than we were in the city.

A razzia, a holdup if you prefer. And I shivered under my jacket.

If you pull it off, Uncle went on, if you pull it off, it will be the absolute perfection of crime. And he'd emphasized each word, like this: the . . . absolute . . . perfection . . . of . . . crime.

We didn't say a thing, Andrei and I, struck speechless, pretending to be taking in all the information (when only a few syllables were sucking up our brains: *ca-si-no, clean-ing out, sur-vi-val, fa-mi-ly*), with our jacket fronts ballooned out over our crossed arms, we coughed just to relieve our uneasiness or something close to it, fear, something divisive that had come among us, is he nuts, I thought about him, about Marin, who'd chewed the idea over on his own, never said one word in front of us, must have persuaded Uncle slowly, quietly, sitting beside him, taking his hand, and promising him, guaranteeing that we'd survive him, that the family would go on without him, and telling us still later: We'll make his name outlive us all. Well, on that point, Marin, I swear to you, you succeeded.

And Uncle kept on talking, looking down at the ground, his gaze sweeping from left to right, back and forth, never daring to confront us, but the tone of his voice expressing confidence in a safe and flawless operation, and the savage will to be done with them, those others. Soon, he insisted, you'll wake up rich, proud, and happy. And the word *casino* was churning through our guts, at Uncle's place, in the car, across the bridge, back at Marin's, that phantom idea behind my narrowed eyes and grimly set lips, because it wasn't for us, the casino, not for the likes of us. People like us, Marin, we operated a notch lower.

Well, maybe we were wiseguys, maybe there was something frightening in our faces, and maybe at one time people in the city were scared of us, of our criminal expertise, our black jackets, maybe we could have kept cruising the shady neighborhoods grabbing any dirty money left lying around, but one thing was certain: the casino—the only way to deal with that was to drive on by with our heads down.

As for escaping it, though, we knew we might as well buy a ticket for Argentina, when we'd already said yes through our silence, according to the time-honored rule in the family whereby a shut trap was a signature on the dotted line. A job like that no thanks, said Andrei, a job like that just when he's going to die soon. But no one in the car wanted to pick up on that, the car reaching the bypass, then the bridge, then the dirt track, and I sensed from Andrei's eyes, Marin's smile, as well as our imminent arrival at his place, at Marin's, that certain impulses to say too much had been nipped in the bud. Then it was so simple to quietly ease the tension with a few remarks meant as red herrings— "I've got to shine my shoes when we get back," "Let's go have a cognac"—and to use them, those little phrases, to change the subject, then forget the whole thing.

As if you could decide on your own to forget, and as if in front of that bay window, at your place, Marin, watching night fall, we'd been able to laugh, to pay attention to the parakeets or look at one another calmly, as if our heads hadn't been cluttered, saturated by that particular thing, that particular job, that December 31 when we'd clean out the casino, that date chosen by Uncle, December 31, because that night the cash boxes will be stuffed with money, Uncle said, and we'll rob them blind, those bastards. New Year's Eve, I felt immediately, would have a bitter taste.

He was quite specific: The last night of the year, it'll be that night and no other. So no one argued, not Marin, not me, not Andrei. Not Jeanne, who'd joined us that evening, because we needed a feminine presence, Uncle had said. He could have said: Because she's your wife, Marin. But what he'd said was: Because we need a woman. And after we'd explained all our plans to her, Jeanne, I remember, she went a bit pale, didn't say anything for a while, then she murmured: He's completely insane. And I replied, with a slight movement of my eyelids, I replied: He's completely insane. But I remember, I didn't know anymore whom I was talking about, Marin, Uncle, me, insane to let ourselves get sucked in like that but not say anything about it, insane to continue, to watch Marin standing in front of his bay window, annoying his parakeets by tapping their cage, to continue drinking together, the two of us, and continue forgetting all that separated us, which was precisely everything—Jeanne, the family, our outlook on the world, the misplaced belief in our plan—but both of us still able, all of a sudden, to kill a bottle together, laugh at the same jokes, and set aside our differences. You, I thought, who spent three years shut up in a cell three yards square, dealing with the overcrowded prison like all the rest of them, no special favors for you, Uncle's pampered nephew. But when you got out of stir, when you came back that night and I saw you come into that club, at the very moment you flattened me I realized that it would all start up again like never before.

And we continued obeying you, getting pissed off of course, keeping an eye on your moods of course, but obeying the entrenched laws of a life lived in common. I often wondered,

Marin, what makes us always bind ourselves to what we hate. But I didn't hate you, Marin, we didn't hate one another, because we belonged to the same family. And that, that family, even in death we'll have to honor it.

So to remain there in that house, just to endure being there, was like pulling a wire taut inside me, in front of him, Marin, his face positively beaming, more open than usual, happier, more serene, all the things that could be read from the unfurrowed brow, the unclenched jaw, the almost jovial eye that jarred with us, Andrei and me, in that spacious living room, with our nerves still on edge from Uncle's orders, his madness, our reticence, our duty, and the feeling of meddling where we didn't belong, overreaching, too big for us, too tough to crack, the coffers of a casino.

Cheers.

Cheers.

Cheers. Our raised glasses punctuated our words, and our eyes, methodically seeking out each face in turn, winking here and there, tried to appear untroubled, or coolly confident. He was almost smiling, Marin, what I mean is, to me it was as if he were smiling, because of the cocksureness, the head held too high, his cigar, the two refills of cognac. I got up quietly, I took the binoculars and looked out into the night at the streetlights shining in the black water on the far side, the deserted port, and I saw, set back from the beach, in close-up I saw the six electric letters, red, spelling out: CASINO. I turned toward Marin, I tried not to blink into the round lenses as he gazed back at me, I even framed each eye in its own circle, saw the enlarged pores on his cheeks, the grog blossoms on his skin, I could almost have felt his breath on my eyes. Behind him, tacked up on the wall like a theatrical backdrop, was the calendar where you could read October 3, Saint Gérard's Day, in huge print, so then I imagined those future mornings with their parade of names, soon it would be Saint Sylvester's turn again, on New Year's Eve. I think I was grinning in the shadow of the binoculars fixed on Marin, his pupils dilated by fever, fatigue, the war gleaming in his eyes, waged against everyone, the whole world within range of his revolver, it seemed, and his yellow parakeets were zipping like tennis balls through my field of vision. Then the rest of us went home, drunk, prolonged farewells, the usual mumblings, see you tomorrow. Tomorrow, because we had to get on track fast.

That was one of Uncle's expressions, to get on track fast and stay there, Uncle used to say, in that fake slangy talk he kept trotting out from under his ratty blanket, a man who still said that you run a city with one hand and with the other you blow the enemy away, the enemy he imagined was still swarming in that miserable milieu of double-crossers, swindlers, and small fry with big mouths, where he was a mythic figure, or a symbol diminished by age.

But what was uppermost in our thoughts, that night, aside from the casino and glowering enemies, aside from the cognac that was slowly befuddling us, what hovered in the deepening night was the abstract space in our minds where Uncle had written in thick letters, *the absolute perfection of crime.*

3

The filthy docks. The rusted rails. The motionless cranes. The creeping desolation. The fog. The quays. The almost gray sea. The breakers. The boardwalk. The bridge in the distance. The highway in the foreground. The red neon sign. The casino.

To get clear images, Andrei explained, you have to hold the camera with both hands, stick your elbows out to either side, and move slowly. The four-lane highway in front. The timing of the lights. The main entrance. The guards like statuettes. The tinted windows.

An ideal view from the ninth floor, he said, there's where you see everything the best on the terrace he'd picked out, and he'd rung the bell of the apartment, where the old lady had let him in. He'd explained to her that he was working for the tourist bureau, producing films to promote the area, and that he was currently looking to showcase the waterfront, the beach, and the casino. She, the old lady, suspicious of course, but giving in of course, had opened her door to him and he'd gone out on her balcony with his camera. And then, when he'd shown us what he called his movie, it had dawned on us, how many obstacles, constraints, fears we'd have to overcome, the massive entrance to the casino, and the highway that went on for so long before we could disappear into the distance.

And they would be valuable, very valuable, all those images, that visual precision, the condescension of the car valet, the class of clients, everything within the silent framework of those shots, zooming in even onto the guards' oily skin and the shine on their shoes. More than valuable, decisive, so much so that we would pattern our actions on that knowledge, visual, cinematic, we said, and avoid hanging around the scene of operations too much. As for sizing up the security, their square jaws, trapezoidal necks, even their jackets seemed to have muscles, so we clearly had to forget about force and rely on cunning.

On cunning, yes, said Marin, I know this kind of place, to get out alive you have to outcheat them. But what we need for that is—a specialist.

I remember, Marin, the day you introduced us to your friend Lucho, a specialist. An old cellmate, he said, a new cousin, if you prefer. Lucho, this is Andrei, and Pierre. And when he stepped toward us, Lucho, when he expected me to hold out my hand to him straight off, with barely enough time to see how he met my eye, I remember, I hesitated, for a good second I hesitated, him in the middle of the room with his hand stuck out, his eyes shifting, looking for Marin, and in the end I stood up, stared at him a moment, and finally gave in, I held out my hand too, and our palms folded around each other, I did it. But frankly, if I had it all to do over again, if only it were possible to replay that scene, I swear to you, Lucho, I'd keep my hand in my pocket.

Because it wasn't enough that we were a fractious family, it wasn't enough that the four of us sat around bored in the blue armchairs, wondering whether the cops or the crooks would take us out, it wasn't enough, settling old accounts among ourselves. His real name was Luciano, but we called him Lucho. It's simpler, said Marin, more like family, and he poured him a cognac.

Lucho didn't drink. Even later, when we went out in the evening, when we made him come along with us, whenever he didn't say "I'm going home" or "I've got work to do," even at night he didn't feel comfortable around bottles. We don't have fun unless we drink, I'd explained to him, otherwise it's like a poker game you've got no money on. Even Marin, he wound up telling Lucho, You have to know how to put part of yourself into things. And you were right, Marin, you have to know how to put part of yourself into things, but sometimes when you put part in, sometimes the rest gets swallowed up as well.

And we initiated him, Lucho—our methods, our operations, the casino. We told him, You see, usually we get rid of people who interfere with our action in the city, but we don't go into their territories, usually, but this, this is different.

The evening when we met, I explained the mailbox business to him. Ordinarily I'd never have said anything, but I was drunk that evening. Marin and I, the mailboxes, they were our favorite activity. When we wanted to eliminate someone, it was very simple, we went into the lobby of his building and ripped his name off his mailbox, then we buzzed him and left. When the guy would come down to see who'd rung his buzzer and spot his name torn off the mailbox, then he knew he was a dead man. Afterward, Marin always said, afterward there are two types of men: the ones who stay home waiting, and the ones who make a break for it. But in either case, Lucho, in either case I swear to you we never missed a one. We liked that job the best, Marin and I.

We asked Lucho what kind of man he'd be, and he answered he'd be the first kind, the ones who wait, of course, because he figured we'd catch the ones who run away. Then we all had a good laugh about it.

The next day, we showed him Andrei's film, in other words everything that was beyond us, the constant surveillance, the guards' psychology, the fear. We showed him why we needed him.

The hardest part, he said, it's not to get ourselves out, but to get out with a bag full of money. All of us in front of the screen, the continuous footage of the casino from all angles, a fortress, we were thinking, an armored cube, so Lucho, when he came out with that, we realized he'd nailed it and we also realized he'd come up with an idea. And he launched right into it: We have to get the money out via the roof.

I remember I didn't dare look at him when he said that, his confident talk, almost his arrogance, it seemed like, projected into the silence that followed. But wait a minute, Marin said, the money has to end up with us, via the roof, what do you mean via the roof?—and he was like a bundle of nerves slamming the wall with his fist, What do you mean via the roof?

Lucho kept his cool, always, and that's how he played him, Marin, that's how he managed him, staying cool. And he explained this idea he had: Via the roof, yes, and we fly the money off. And turning toward the outdoors, looking at the overcast sky on that gray morning, he let us listen as time strolled by, he turned back to us, and he said: A hot-air balloon, a miniature dirigible, a balloon operated by remote control, lands on the roof, one of us puts the money in, it takes off, and we bring it back wherever we want.

First we burst out laughing. We imagined the newspaper headlines: Hot-Air Holdup, Boodle in a Balloon, High-Altitude Heist. We imagined the money in a gondola sailing above buildings, dangling in the fresh sea breeze of New Year's Eve. We imagined the guards below, standing outside the casino, with their reason for being there flying off over their heads. Lucho started to act out the scene, imitating the guards.

You hear something?

No, you, you hear something?

No, nothing. And you?

Nothing. Okay, let's go back to sleep.

He played both parts, Lucho, mimicked their gestures and their big blank stares, had us in stitches, even Marin, he broke up, and I saw the pride in his eyes, as if his intuition had paid off for all to see, in the intelligence of his new recruit, Lucho, who was yet so different from us, since he was so far outside the family.

And immediately we wrote on a sheet of paper: Get the money out via the roof with a balloon. Because we wrote down everything, notes, ideas, sketches. Things written down, we said, belong to all of us, as if the paper, from notepads advertising brands of cognac, had managed to absorb our personal pride, as if one syllable, one letter from each idea set down there, on paper, belonged to each of us, and we could claim in common those witty remarks shooting through the smoky atmosphere of the living room, freeing it for a moment from an oppressive weariness, giving us the illusion that we believed in the plan. So, a hot-air balloon, and getting the money out via the roof. Did you believe in it, Marin, really?

But when Lucho came up from the basement a few weeks later, from the workshop, he called it, that he'd set up for himself down there, came up in more of a hurry than usual, more disheveled than usual, his eyes reddened from the strain of the electric light, the detail work, the obsession, when he emerged from his downstairs workshop, we knew right away that he'd pulled it off.

That same damn guy who'd popped up out of nowhere a month before, Lucho, little by little he'd brought his new "family" to heel, demanding from them, Marin above all, total isolation, since underground seclusion was appropriate for a craftsman, Marin said, and we shouldn't worry about him. So when we saw him smiling, leaning on the handrail of the staircase, we just parked our drinks right there on the floor and followed him down to the basement. All the parts were spread out on the ground: a large, clumsily folded piece of blue cloth, to which were attached almost invisible lengths of fishing line, joined in turn to a small wicker gondola, as big as and remarkably like a laundry basket.

The inflated fabric balloon, he assured us, had a diameter no larger than five feet but was capable of lifting a basket twice as large into the air. And we hoped to see it soon, this basket, filled with something more exciting than dirty clothes. I remember as well how you looked at us, Marin, with Lucho grinning like a kid who's invited his parents into his room.

But the next night we were all of us kids, sitting on the sand watching it fly, the blue balloon. Carried here and there by the wind, it was almost invisible in the misty night sky, rising, falling, vanishing into the void above our heads tipped back so our eyes could follow, necks craning at its every whim, meaning the whims of the breeze that wafted it around, the balloon, even though it wasn't very strong, the wind, that evening of the first trial flight. But what would happen in a storm, I asked, if the night of the thirty-first were windy, to the balloon, and the money? Nothing serious, Lucho replied, we'd just have to row a bit farther to pick it up.

To row, yes, because he'd proposed as well, Lucho, to have the money drop onto the sea, in the outer harbor, where the lights of the city fade away. A primary precaution, he explained, not too many enemies at sea, one of us just needs to go get the balloon out on the water. And I pictured the choppy waves and having to manage the unbearably frail boat, the hull skidding into the troughs, shooting into the air at the top of each crest. There are currents, I said, even in the roadstead, even a long way from the wild water of the open sea.

The thirty-first will not be a stormy night, announced Marin abruptly. And what joy on each face, a delight that was obvious even in the dark, we went home happy to have scored a point at this stage of our operation, some notable progress, we'd agree over our cognac, for a change.

For a change we'd wind up believing it would work, especially as we could no longer see ourselves turning back, in other words, as we settled into our roles as armed robbers. How poorly those words suited us, armed robbers. Even Marin, so gung ho, had winced at that description, when I put my foot in it one evening, looking off toward the port, toward the casino, blurting out those words that almost made us feel ashamed: armed robbers. But later, not right away, but later, he reacted, Marin, one night he said wearily: Don't you ever say that again. I barely remembered making that crack, but him, he'd been mulling it over in the meantime. With our hair so nicely combed, our jackets so nicely tailored, he would have liked us, naturally, to answer to a different definition than armed robbers. Gangsters or wiseguys, fine, but not armed robbers. And that night I thought he'd go out of control again, get violent again, but he didn't. Because as the day of reckoning approached, on the contrary he calmed down, eased off on his drinking, lowered his voice at the end of his sentences, and stopped teasing his parakeets to make them squawk.

Even at Uncle's place, he didn't pace in front of the window anymore, talking constantly and fogging up the glass, but now sat in the creaking chair at the foot of the bed, his elbows resting on his knees, head bowed over his clasped hands, only his eyes from time to time showing pity for Uncle's jaundiced skin, waiting for him to die.

4

But it didn't change a thing that he died. It didn't change a thing for you. You didn't even cry.

The morning of the funeral, the only thing he found to do, Marin, was to write D-day 30 on the wall calendar. D-day 30, he noted with a felt-tip, because he'd decided that from now on we needed a countdown to motivate us. I thought it over this morning, he said, that from today on we'd count off the days. Him up since dawn, like always smoking in front of his bay window since dawn, because he didn't sleep much, and every morning he made fun of our sleeping late, our puffy eyes when we showed up at around ten, eleven o'clock, it depended on the night before, meaning the cognac. But that morning, the effort we'd made, Andrei and I, to be spruce and clean-shaven in our funeral suits, that morning, all he found to say was, the days left would be clearly marked off. Even the sky was gloomy, but not him.

He'd died two days earlier, Uncle, which made it D-day 32. And we couldn't tell anymore, that December 1, where the exhaustion was coming from, from overdoing it night after night, or from the day ahead of us. The ceremony was scheduled for three that afternoon, a religious ceremony, Catholic, a man who all his life had spat on religion, on Catholics, had at the last moment wanted a religious burial, had begged Auntie to arrange a place for him in the family vault. He'd insisted on having a plaque installed: "Lived in the world, died in the Church."

We reached Auntie's place around noon. Marin prepared the coffee, no one said much. The occasional glance into the living room at the casket, still open. It hasn't made much of a change, I thought, in his familiar position: hands folded over his abdomen, eyes closed, it's just that we don't hear him breathing anymore, because his lungs have stopped. The big book with the burgundy cover was wedged near one hip, in the coffin, and would remain there, Auntie had said. She's the one who poured our coffee, and she sat down with us. So then in the quiet chill of that noon, of the funereal wait that made us still believe we were a "family," I couldn't help myself, I launched the discussion, or lanced the abscess, saying in front of everyone, We don't have any reason to do it anymore, we don't have any reason to do it now that he's dead.

I'd worked that sentence up in my mind, hoping it wouldn't peter out along the way, that my voice would carry it through to the end, and then my chest did tighten up a little, because Marin was in front of me, like a mirror shoved in my face. I'd have liked to look at them all one at a time, time enough for each one to admit the obvious, that maybe we had nothing more to do together, but my eyes, my lips, my breath, everything was directed at Marin. Jeanne, Auntie, Andrei, they were momentarily shut out of the scene.

And naturally it was Marin who reacted. He said nothing of course, he took a long, deep breath, sat back in his chair, but said nothing. He got up slowly and went into the living room, past the coffin. Stood at the window and looked outside, hands clasped behind his back. The rest of us had no idea what violence or gentleness might come of this, what role you would choose to invent in front of us, in front of Jeanne perhaps, and Auntie. But I swear to you, Marin, we no longer had any reason to act.

The silence spread throughout the house, even to the garden, to the tired apple trees. It was Andrei's turn to sigh. Andrei stood up despite the fear and said it was true, the whole thing had been completely crazy from the beginning, the casino had never been our kind of business, and now absolutely, now that Uncle was dead, it didn't make sense anymore, it was preposterous. He stumbled over the first *p* in *preposterous,* as though he stuttered or his voice in particular had hesitated, and Marin turned back toward us, he went around the coffin in the other direction, he leaned against the wall, framed by the doorway, and on his face, like a veil, most unusual, was a faint tremor. Jeanne went up to him, slipped her arm behind his back. She was like a screen between him and us. But she didn't know either, Jeanne, whether she ought to kiss him or run away from him, because his face at that moment, it was like a foreign language. Jeanne most of all, usually so sensitive to his mood, divining the state of his soul, at a loss this time, she waited to see what would happen. But he didn't break down, Marin, he didn't weep over Uncle's coffin, he didn't invoke the "family," or pull a gun, he didn't curse anyone out, didn't even use the word "traitors," he smiled instead, smiled sweetly to steady his nerves, and we settled for going along with that.

You should have cried, Marin. But you were already far away, looking at Uncle laid out in the wood of his coffin, following the black van along the winding roads, you were already a long way away from "family" business. So happy after all to see the marble slab close over Uncle, in front of the twenty, thirty people who'd knelt for the occasion before the tomb. So satisfied to breathe the fossilized ancestral air, count the number of levels inside the vault again and reassure yourself, knowing your spot was all ready. From that moment on you were almost eager to join him.

We followed the cortege. Marin and I led off, Auntie between us, holding on to our arms, and only the coffin in front of us, carried by six men bearing the mass of ebony, without any jolts or sudden stops, in that solemn and silent funeral march we felt we were conducting in spite of ourselves, Marin and I, because of the family relationship generally assumed, which earned us that prime place, ahead of everyone. But even before that day, Marin, long before that day, we could have walked behind the coffin. We made it through the condolence line, the stream of sorrowful faces, then the umbrellas tagging along behind us, like several yards of black bombs, how many of them had followed all the way to the cemetery to hear that distinctive scraping of the slab or that other strange noise, the crunch of their shoes on the gravel. And how many had left us at the church, having fulfilled what might have seemed like a civic duty, in the large chapel that had easily welcomed the perhaps 120, 150 people who'd first thronged at the doors, then bowed their heads, then gone home again.

Last homage rendered to that now and forever cold, stiff old man who had represented, in a certain society, the priest had said, a prominent person, an undeniable presence whose long life had managed to overcome the terrible pitfalls of a complex, tumultuous destiny, and whom the Lord would know how to recognize as one of His own.

But for a long time, dear Uncle, you'd been nothing more than a shadow. A shadow of himself, they murmured in that certain society, that provincial Mafia. So now there'd be no more using the intercom at the front gate, no more tramping along the path edged with nettles and brambles, when arriving at Uncle's, and now the word "family," in everyone's minds, would come equipped with its quotation marks.

He'd been born ninety-two years ago, in 1899, and to hear them some people took pleasure, solace, and pride in pronouncing that date and elevating their own souls, especially Marin, who'd always seemed to grow larger from seeing that body every week, that ruin of flesh and blood serving as a link to the previous century. 1899, he'd say, pausing so deliberately afterward you couldn't help but look quickly away so that finally even the shortest silence carried great weight. Would 1899 be engraved on the tomb? And when I think back on it, Marin, when I think back on it, I'd like to stuff those four numbers down your throat.

And sometimes I dream—that inscrutable look in your eyes—I dream of clenching your hair in my fist, of flattening your nose there, in front of me, in front of Auntie, who's pressed flat against the epitaph.

The feeling that came over me when they moved the stone, those different levels inside, it was like a dormitory at summer camp, and what kept me from going in myself, I can't say today if it was the desire to live or the silence in there, but the supposed eternity of those who had been placed there ten, fifteen, thirty years before, that eternity being offered to Uncle, for one moment it made me jealous. Amen, came a chorus of sighs. Amen.

The sadness lingered on that evening. Marin seemed to be still gazing into the grave, but it wasn't grief, Andrei said, just what had happened at noon. And it was Andrei who spoke up again, he said it was only sadness that had made us think of giving up, that we were going to pull it off, that job, and soon we'd be rich, the "family" would be rich and we'd be able to carry on. But his share, Marin, if he'd had to decide that instant what to do with it, he'd have thrown it out the bay window, and himself along with it. I imagined his body floating out in the harbor, his livid face plastered with soggy bills, drifting among the waves, and deep inside, I laughed.

5

Every day that went by, we told ourselves, we could have just dropped the whole thing, but what made us stay on course and keep going all out, I admit, as we already wondered at the time, Andrei and I especially, we didn't know. A sad clutch of hours spent harping on the absurdity of the situation, being bored behind Marin's windows and looking at that sky so gray, or so dreary, which had condensed for us into one single sensation. When the fog rolled in or the sky grew overcast, all you could see through the bay window was the trees, as if in that outdoors, with the sea spray and the city in the distance behind it, when the sun wasn't shining only the chlorophyll color braved the transparency of the glass to cast a cloud over our souls, first over the walls, then by extension, over our souls. We were like kids when there was drizzle or grayness, if we'd been younger it would have made us feel suicidal, a few times, because of the cracks opening up in our hearts, because of that rain or the trees that were too green and seemed to vomit all over us, we'd get restless, work poorly, and we'd long for the night so we could drown our distress in it.

Because we weren't about to give up going out at night in

contrast to our days, showing ourselves in the city come evening, black jackets, hair properly combed, scented, we'd sit on the high stools, elbows on the bar, and feel watched, in other words, respected. How many times we'd wind up our nights there, where we ran into the same old faces, in that club called the Lord Jim. Another reason we went there, because Uncle had owned it.

At the Lord Jim we retold old stories, settled old accounts, drank to be friends. One cognac then another, Marin would order for himself, then another and another, when we bellied up to the bar next to him, and cognac after cognac, so would we. And always sitting up straight in spite of the alcohol, and the waning hours, and the mauve couches we'd be parked on at dawn. Our hearty laughter, our bluff camaraderie. When you get right down to it, Marin, that's the only place where we ever felt so close, so friendly, like brothers.

A last cognac, we'd propose after four o'clock, when the bartender had already put the chairs up on the tables and was mechanically swishing his broom nearby, one last round please Yann, so Yann would slip back behind the bar, reach into his cupboards and pull out his special bottle, knowing that before we left he had his debt to pay, like a tax levied on the spot, one worth as much as all the handshakes in the world.

In seven years we'd become kings, since the now so distant day when we'd met Uncle, in that same dark hangout that blotted up our nights, that man who for some reason had welcomed us, him, Uncle, already so old. But we didn't call him that, either Uncle or monsieur or anything, we never even thought to shake his hand. For some obscure reason we followed him into his office, Marin and I in front of the whiskey bottle, that's what we drank at the time, whiskey, only later moving on to cognac, that's for old guys we used to say, we followed him, Uncle, and never left him when at dawn in front of the empty bottle he said: You just have to learn not to drink so fast. But that, even seven years later, we still hadn't learned how to do.

Even seven years later, nightfall, the alcohol it brought and its indifference to the day's troubles, that was still what put us back on our feet. Often, after watching the same falling rain, the same befogged rust in the backdrop of the harbor, the same faraway streetlamps glistening across the sea, we'd go out, Marin and I especially, pretending to be satisfied with our day, our assigned tasks, and I'd act as if I believed in it a bit more, in what doubt was undermining, sabotaging, chipping away, that pathetic project, the casino robbery, because we should have given up on the whole thing, on Uncle, on Lucho, on everything, from the beginning.

Even Uncle, in his last weeks, seemed to have withdrawn, on those awful Saturday mornings, during those long monologues in which Marin kept reviewing everything, laying it all out, Marin couldn't get over the fact that we'd hit a snag, he said, worse than ramming a tree trunk on a river. It's just that basically, Marin my friend, Uncle didn't give a fuck for your wacko projects, since everything seemed unimportant to him and too far from his bed. Even when we explained the whole plan in detail, meaning how we were going to get inside the casino, our escape routes or the place we'd picked for our fallback rendezvous, even the division of the haul, he didn't give a fuck.

Even that strange day when we brought Lucho to meet him, his almost amazement, Lucho, at being introduced to an old man, brought into the fold, constantly smiling, but when he and Marin went over to the bed, the old man, eyes perfectly closed, never even twitched a muscle, he simply said: Do whatever you want, Marin, whoever you want, you're a big boy now. And there'd been something black, nauseating, repugnant about it, as if our collective drowning, the collapse that was already so visible, as if Uncle had orchestrated it, prophesied it for himself, and were leaving us on our own. That day, Andrei and I wound up going out to the orchard, idly kicking a few of the overripe apples on the ground, exchanging two three meaningless glances before heading back toward the house, trampling the pale and monotonous lichens on the front stoop, then kissing Auntie and Uncle good-bye, as usual. Even the wink Uncle gave me that time when I embraced him, I never knew if it was a conscious gesture, a nervous reflex, or both.

So to find ourselves out under the autumn sky driving around the casino, letting ourselves be dazzled by the six letters in red neon on the facade—I still wonder, Marin, why you wanted to save us. Us, the family, Uncle, the man who if he'd lived wouldn't have made anything of it all except one more trophy, an umpteenth and final notch on his gun. And I should have prayed in particular that it wouldn't be my stuffed head gracing his walls as a prize, so convinced was I right up to the end that the whole thing was too much for us.

Even during those long weeks before the action, driving on the highway that hugged the ground below the casino, we constantly checked through the rear windshield, from behind the protection of the For Sale sign, making sure the headlights of a car marked Police would not, ever, get close to us. What Andrei said was, They can smell us a long way off, because we're sweating fear, and fear leads to more fear that leads to screwups, he'd fume, almost like a man condemned to death and fighting for the hell of it against what's bound to happen anyway, no matter how hard he cries. Tireless inspectors of our own tracks, more suspicious than any squad of zealous policemen, how we wished we could have cloned ourselves, and sent our shadows to replace us on the thirty-first while we were far away, at the movies, or a fancy restaurant. What we'd have liked most of all was to get our hands on the money without even having to set foot in the casino, but soon we'd be caught from head to toe in the bright lights of the gaming tables.

6

While we're at it, I said one evening, all we have to do is disguise ourselves as convicts, we'll save some time. But nobody laughed, me neither, actually, when I'd looked again at the dwindling calendar: D-day 2. Even Lucho, he finally said that if everything went wrong we'd know why, and he really didn't appreciate my always chasing after bad luck.

We stayed with our dark suits until the last evening, our shirts buttoned up to the collar, our jackets that seemed to get blacker as the nights got longer. The day before, we started playing cards, poker, for money. To keep our minds off it, Lucho said. To keep Marin's mind off it, I thought, because Lucho was a psychologist. Because in prison they'd gotten to know each other. Because in a cell three yards square, you can't avoid getting to know your cellmate. And because the two of them, I also thought, they didn't meet up by chance, then I staked a hundred francs on the table and stopped thinking. We played for two hours, winning and losing in turn. We drank each time we bet and wound up pretty drunk, except for Lucho.

Even Jeanne, she drank too much that evening, Jeanne, so restrained, never judging or commenting on our activities, placid, she was, she'd have to be to put up with our behavior, yours especially, Marin, your violence, your mood swings, Andrei said. But she was so tired as well, she finally broke down, collapsing on the table and insulting each one of us, losers, she called us, she wanted nothing to do with a bunch of losers, she'd go find others, even worse losers, we should just leave her alone now, and go fuck ourselves. She said she wasn't going to go play the whore at the casino.

But you weren't anything like a whore, Jeanne, at the casino. And in the department stores trying on the clothes, the outfits we'd wear for our losers' game at the casino, it was something else, Jeanne, I swear. A whole afternoon having a ball like kids in the fluorescent lights, the suits, I'd take five or six for the fitting room, come out all spiffy, Jeanne waiting for me behind the curtain, checking me out in detail, then she'd laugh, or make a face, or clap her hands, until I wound up with a jacket, matching pants, bow tie. When I came out of the fitting room for the fifth time, all in black with a white shirt, she didn't say anything, Jeanne. Did I look a little like a pimp? And the escalator to the women's floor, winding our way through the lingerie, the little-old-lady blouses, running her hand lightly over everything, and I was telling her, That would look nice on you, that skirt, those panty hose, that coat, that would look nice on you, that one there. Her turn to emerge from the fitting room. A long white gown, luminous, to me it was like a vision, and I repeat, Jeanne, anything but a whore. She stood there in front of me and asked me if I liked it, that white dress, but I couldn't say a word. Of course I liked it, of course Jeanne, but even saying it wouldn't have come close, and I nodded but that's all.

Marin will like it, I thought.

How many times I asked myself whatever could have pushed her, Jeanne, into his arms, what lightning must strike people head over heels sometimes, Jeanne who so often had trouble smiling, who for three years went to see him twice a week, who waited outside the door even before it opened and never missed a visit in three years, and Marin who so quickly forgot to thank her for it.

You often forgot to thank people, Marin.

And that evening when he told her to go to bed, when he said Go to bed now—it pissed me off. I was drunk too, tired too, so when I heard that, the two of us facing each other across the table, when I heard that I said: I'm coming over there. He opened his eyes wide, stared at me and burst out laughing. I said it again: I'm coming over there. Now. Then I put down my cards and went over to him, he kept laughing and sputtering over his cigar, I raised my hand and walloped the side of his head. There was a dull sound, there was the movement of his head bending down with the force of the blow, there was Jeanne yelling. You say that again, Marin, you ever talk like that again, and I'll make you eat your parakeets. So now he gets up, naturally, but he didn't come at me right away, he went over to the cage first, and he caught a bird in his hand, the parakeet was practically smothered, I backed up until I was against the wall, and in front of me he's ready, brings the parakeet up to my mouth: You'll eat it before I do, he said. Jeanne was still yelling, she ran over to us, her fists started pounding on Marin's back, so eventually he let the bird fly off and he sat back down at the table.

In a way, I've thought since, nothing happened that evening, but family tragedy that night in December, we only just missed it, by the skin of our teeth, I was that close to pulling my piece on Marin, because of Jeanne, or Uncle, or the cognac, because of everything that would sometimes make you stretch a rope or open your veins, I came so close. But I didn't do it, that's my lookout.

7

D-day. Afternoon at my place. Coffee still hot. My face in the mirror. Nap in the armchair. At two that afternoon, I turned on the TV. At three, I shaved. At four, I settled into the impossibility of sleep. Solitude. Each of us privately going over privately the logical series of actions, privately. The boredom beforehand, the dry cold, the clear sky framed in the windows. At two, I turned on the TV. At three, I shaved. At four, I settled into the impossibility of sleep. At five, I went out, I ran a few errands, bought some oranges, apples, red wine. At six, I lay down on my bed, hands behind my head. At seven, I took something for my nerves, with a large glass of water. Then I almost fell asleep. But it was time to meet the others.

Part Two

....

I

Around nine o'clock, Marin gave it a heave, and the dull gray warehouse door rolled up on its tracks. We slipped inside, first glancing up and down the alley, a precaution, or a habit, like many things we would now do without knowing anymore if they were prompted by reason or instinct. Marin, Jeanne, and I were first, but Lucho, then Andrei wouldn't be long, punctuality being a major factor that day, although we closed the door behind us anyway. It gets dark early at that time of the year; Marin groped for the switch, found it, and said, Let there be light. Maybe he said it ironically, I don't know, I didn't see any irony or humor in his eyes, then we went to the center of the warehouse where a table, five chairs, and three crates were the only furniture, gathered together awaiting our return since the previous evening when we'd brought everything there, the crates of stuff set down in the darkness, so late at night even the cries of seagulls spooked us. Marin and I sat facing each other at the round table, the cold chairs scraped on the concrete, the lightbulb dangling from the ceiling swung between us, hanging like a man's head about to slip from its noose, glaring in both our faces. I coughed to clear my throat, or fill the silence, I don't know anymore. The door screeched again, opened halfway to let them in, Lucho, then Andrei. You'd have thought they'd agreed to meet outside, their shadows stretched out by the only streetlight around, and their bodies putting on flesh and dimension inside. It was a moonless night. A clear and firm decision from way back, that date of the thirty-first, but from the beginning we'd made sure there'd be no moon that evening, no trail of light, Marin had said, there'll be enough of a trail without that, Uncle had said. Andrei shut the battered metal door, we hugged one another hard, a little shakily, too.

It was 9:02 when Marin checked his watch. He didn't need to say anything, all our actions from then on had been perfectly planned and rehearsed. Talking, we'd agreed, was just useless repetition, we didn't need such reassurance. Marin bent over one of the crates and pulled out four revolvers, placing one stiffly on the table in front of each of us except Jeanne. It would have been too bad if Jeanne had had to carry a gun, that's for sure, given the dress she'd be wearing an hour later—where would she have hidden it anyway, a revolver, or even a nail file, and from where I sat, she'd be magnificent in her white gown, an hour later. Next the clips, two apiece, likewise placed in front of us, kept in sight for the moment, the guns to be tucked away in our waistbands, one clip already loaded, the other in the inside jacket pocket, and we'd leave. But first, Marin set out five liqueur glasses bought for the occasion and christened them with a bottle of cognac.

We all five clinked glasses, leaving no one out. With five of us, the rims tapped ten times in the empty air, echoing the contact ten times to reflect how we were bound together, then we knocked back the cognac, *Cuvée spéciale holdup,* said Marin with a smile, still sitting, then silent. We looked into one another's eyes, each of us wondering how the others felt, still in silence. In my memory the scene lasted an hour, but in reality, five minutes, the alcohol, the concrete, the frowns, and our glances pulling tight the drawstring of our fear. We waited. We no longer knew for what, or for what sign or gesture, we were waiting. I thought the five of us could have encouraged and hugged one another, I've since thought that we should have done that, but it was already clear that we were each far away from the faces across the table. Jeanne tried to smile at me, and held back. She wanted to, I saw that in the movement of her eyes, but she caught herself, she looked down at the bottle in the center of the table, and that was that. And the idea that we were supposed to meet there again in three hours—well that just seemed like eternity to me, to all of us. I stared a long while at the bottle thinking, with the revolver lying on the wooden table, that we were heading right for a wall, but charging ahead anyway. Jeanne was wearing her serene expression. Marin his edgy one. In such moments, you yourself even forget to worry about what kind of impression you're making. So much the better in a way, I've told myself since then, because a mirror at a time like that would be worse than a slug in the gut. And yet we were used to those moments of stage fright, but that time it was different, and the bitterness was there, low-lying, like the grit on the floor. We do nothing unwillingly, after all, nothing. Still, we had another round, no one refused, not even Lucho, usually sober as a judge, that evening he tipped back the second glass just as fast and didn't lift his hand to say, enough. An expression crossed my mind, something like "It's chilly tonight," the way I might have thought "An angel passes" in the awkward lull, the same degree of absurdity, of nervous nonsense bothering us, inclining us to silence. We had the right to cough, the right to smoke noisily, to spit on the floor, to shuffle our feet under the table, but not to talk too much. Just action, we'd said that practically from the beginning, action even when we spoke.

9:15 and while we'd been marking time in our thoughts, the time had come to prepare for real: our outfits, our tools, our accessories—Marin and I reached deep into the crates and pulled out polished shoes, hooks, ropes, glasses, knives, a makeup case, flashlights. Andrei was jingling the keys to the van, the noise echoing around the sheet-metal space of the warehouse, and when I shot him a look he stopped immediately. Then from his back pocket Marin pulled an envelope folded in half: sixty thousand francs, right out of the night.

Sixty thousand francs, that was the amount to be spent in the plan we'd come up with, the act we would stage in the casino, Jeanne and I, since we were supposed to pass for very rich people, play roulette for half an hour, and lose the money as quickly as possible, so that we could then make a scene, it was part of the plan. Jeanne was sort of like the Trojan horse. So, sixty thousand francs, because to win big you have to know how to spend big, I cracked. But it's true, it's true, yelled Marin, as if trying to justify himself, as if at that moment we'd seen the sixty thousand vanishing before our eyes, when we were supposed to rake in a hundred times as much, but fear, or the cost of failure spelled out in heavy francs in front of us, sent a shiver through the humid air. And Marin still at it: You want to divvy it up, go ahead, everyone gets a New Year's present, you can have my share, it's easier to divide sixty thousand by four than by five. But we didn't want to hear or pick up on that and began getting ready, our bare feet on the cold, rough concrete; I unpacked the last accessories from the crate: the cane for my disguise, the mirror to see how we looked, the false papers for Jeanne and me, just in case. Andrei was now pacing back and forth, clenching the keys in his hand, and not daring to say anything, either, because Andrei, he had the beauty part, as Marin's driver. No need for him to face the *Good evenings* of the casino gorillas, or the suspicion of the gaming-room supervisors. He'd be the one driving the C15 and waiting not far from the casino, ready to hit the horn and the gas if trouble showed up.

Lucho watched us, still in his seat and a full glass in front of him, he'd poured himself another refill, I noticed, but I hadn't time to think about that. I straightened the bow tie on my white shirt, Marin stood up to fasten his big ankle boots and stared at me, he in a dark warm-up suit, I in my tuxedo, and despite his smile to hide the uneasiness, I felt the hitch, the mental pause, because of the contrast at that moment, not between the risks to be taken, but between classes, the class division. While I was going to play a golden boy who blows his wad on roulette, he'd act the part of the thug who deals in pure action, that's how it was, scripted like that, and my face surely betrayed compassion, the thought that we'd decided correctly, but that we'd never have the same talents. And he certainly deciphered in me, in the little glasses I'd just carefully put on, deciphered line by line each hidden feeling, amazing how our whole history was there, I thought, in the unequal distribution of our roles. Okay, he said, check your watches. 9:25 for everyone, and in five minutes the door would glide up again, then down, the five of us would already have encouraged one another with a hug, a pat on the back, a "Here goes shit" muttered for luck. Five minutes more to review the sequence of events in our heads, each of us on his or her own track, the possible getaways, five minutes to clear our heads of any deeper meaning or valid reason or motivation lagging far behind us at that moment. And I don't know anymore whether it was shadows or wild animals that left the warehouse that evening, but I do know that for a while, for certain, we had distanced ourselves from the idea of humanity.

It was all tightly organized, what we had to do and when we had to do it, for weeks we'd worked to minimize the risks, to parameterize, as they say, the situation, to attain what would forever be called the absolute perfection of crime. And the door slid open one last time. Outside, one behind the other, the C15 van and the Mercedes were parked in the darkness. We referred to the van as the cattle truck, a metal cage more than a car, because there were no seats in the back. We'd each already had the pleasure of sitting right on the metal floor, wickedly shaken by the slightest touch on the brakes, dreading potholes, railroad tracks, speed bumps, and we usually made fun of whoever had to ride there. But that evening, I swear, when Andrei slammed the rear doors shut behind Lucho, who was half drunk and peering through the window like an animal locked in a kennel, we didn't feel like laughing, didn't even think about laughing, and neither did he, Lucho, with only an old scrap of carpet to cushion his bones, he didn't even smile. Andrei got behind the wheel, Marin got in beside him, and the van backed up to the corner of the road. I slipped behind the wheel of the Mercedes, with Jeanne in the front passenger's seat. In the rearview mirror I saw my eyes shining as I stared ahead at the back end of the van, I flipped down the center armrest, my skull sank into the padded seat-back, and in the rearview mirror again I was aware of the solid mass of the warehouse falling away behind us. It was the only place, we'd decided early on, where we'd be left alone at night, especially that night, because we'd figured the outskirts would be deserted, dead, emptied of the few activities that drew visitors, there where even the dregs of society, the newspapers said, no longer risked going, so far away did that area seem from the world of the living. And it was there, to that world of the living, that we were heading that evening at sixty miles an hour.

On the highway we passed the C15, as planned. As planned, Andrei would drop Lucho off in front of his apartment building, meaning the one where he'd be working with the balloon, but we'll get to that later. As planned, Andrei and Marin would drive on to the rendezvous point. We were already there,

Jeanne and I, at the rendezvous, when we saw the C15's head-lights appear in front of us, the beams jarred by the bumpy road leading to where we waited, barely two hundred yards from the casino, both of us leaning against the doors of the Mercedes and chain-smoking cigarette after cigarette. It was 9:50. The engine was cut, the van's headlights went out, and in the darkness we could see Jeanne's white dress still glimmering from the after-glow. Then that fleeting whiteness also died, leaving only the in-candescent ashes of our cigarettes in the blackness, the crisp slam of the van door, and Marin's voice commenting on the temper-ature, rather chilly that night.

At 10:00 Jeanne and I were to take our same places in the Mercedes, and I would drive to the front entrance. There, the car valet would open the doors for us and park the car, while Marin was to get up to the third floor via the balconies. Jeanne and I would settle at a roulette table, like a wealthy young couple on their honeymoon or something like that, while he would scale the building, as I said, then saw through the metal of a barred window to get inside a staff rest room, then fifteen minutes to knock out the alarm systems, then he'd rejoin me, near the eleva-tor, at exactly 10:35. Only then would we make our move. Jeanne would continue her dainty-doll act at the roulette table throughout the entire operation, with the extra ten thousand francs we'd leave her so she could entertain everyone, so all eyes would be on her, seeing how magnificent she was, in her white dress.

2

Do what you did on the day of the events, the judge said. The scene had to begin outside, at the moment Jeanne and I arrived in the black Mercedes and pulled up in front of the main entrance. For the reconstruction we don't need the girl, they said, and you'll act as though she were here. The cops had parked the car a short way down the street, to make it seem as if I were coming straight from the warehouse, except that I was really coming straight from prison. I saw the time on a policeman's watch, it was 10:00 P.M. I climbed out of the police van, handcuffed, blinded by the flashbulbs, there was an incredible mob, journalists, the curious, an uproar. You could sense the crowd behind the barriers, and the circle of cops protecting the area. I thought I glimpsed Marin's face in the throng, a few times, then I forgot about it. They led me to the Mercedes, the judge stood there with his bullhorn, Okay here we go he said, and one of the cops asked me to get behind the wheel. They cleared the street and I drove to the main entrance of the casino, up to the steps, I set the brake, and handed the keys to the car valet. It was him, the same one who had in fact parked the car on the thirty-first, it was to him that I handed the keys for the second time. And he played along, same gesture he made fifty times a night, opened the car door for me, wished me a good evening, held out his hand. I tried to find the same face I'd had that night, to smile at him in the same way, to place the money for his tip in his hand with the same dexterity and the same condescension, those of a man who'd done that all his life. And my heart, my pulse—gradually I found the same excitement again, the same mixed intoxication as I climbed the steps, as if we were going to pull the same con, as if Jeanne were holding my arm and smiling at everyone. The camera flashes kept lighting up the night. I crossed the lobby with a nod to the security goons at the entrance, I entered the gaming room, slowly, and I went over to table number 4. Everything was just as it had been, people at every table, the tuxedos, the ties, the jewelry at the women's throats. They'd gone all out to make it similar, the atmosphere, the quiet hysteria, the artificial politeness of the croupiers. If there hadn't been three cops and a judge behind me, if there hadn't been a jumpy guy dancing around me taking photos every ten seconds, I'd have sworn that I'd really come back. For an instant I felt Jeanne next to me, and I felt our solitude in that huge room, beneath those grand chandeliers, the same feeling I'd had on the thirty-first, so I'd made a detour to the bar, and I'd ordered a whiskey. The words had come naturally, a whiskey, not a cognac, while Jeanne, I remember, she had a gin and grapefruit. After that, more relaxed, we'd strolled over to table number 4.

At that point the judge interrupted the action, asking me if I was sure that it was really that table, number 4, the one where people were playing roulette, if in fact I'd sat down there as confidently as I had this time around. I replied that yes, that maybe as far as confidence was concerned, it was easier this second time in his presence, sad to say, because that reassured me in a way, because this time there wasn't the fear that it would all go wrong, I said. He smiled at me, and told me to continue. And so I continued, placed my white scarf on the back of the chair, nodded a few times, and bet a chip, then two, then ten. They gave me everything I asked for, the sixty thousand francs I'd had with me on the thirty-first, they handed them to me as well, not fake money, real bills, so that I could play the same game.

So, the night of the events, we'd lost money quite quickly as planned, meaning that we placed the riskiest bets to have the smallest chance of winning, because the night of the events, we had to lose the sixty thousand francs to win a hundred times more, had to start losing them fast so as to make the requisite fuss as soon as possible and make the fuss, on the contrary, last as long as possible, with me slowly and steadily losing my temper, so that I would attract everyone's attention, first table 4, then the neighboring tables, at last the whole casino, so that security would get involved. So that then the director himself would come down from his office, discuss the situation with me, apologizing, so that I could wangle a private talk with him, upstairs, and then, in his office, I'd have a free hand. And therefore, during the reconstruction, I was supposed to lose the money in the same way, so I did what I'd done on the big evening, I bet two three times to make things look normal, then I bet twenty-five thousand on the 36, in other words I had one chance in thirty-six of winning. I bet on the 36 with the sole purpose of losing that money immediately. There were lots of people around the table, chips circulating in all directions, placed on the table, odd, black, manque, everyone was caught up in the game. Even the cops standing behind me, they watched the action feverishly. The croupier was about to spin the wheel, *rien ne va plus, mesdames messieurs, rien ne va plus,* and he set it going. The ball tripped along the circle of numbers for a long while, running around the wheel several times before stopping, not at all anxious to make up its mind, everyone was watching me, tense, excited, all the light seemed focused on my table, concentrated there for me, brightening my eyes, the croupier's too, the little ball wavered right to the end, the 1, the 36, the 1, and finally the 36. The same 36 I'd bet on. I closed my eyes. Sweat pearled on my face, the croupier looked at me, he was flabbergasted, his eyes were popping. Then he became upset. Seemed almost to pity me. And I caught myself imagining what would have happened if I had actually won on December 31. Twenty-five thousand on the 36, that's 36 times twenty-five thousand francs, in other words if I'd won nine hundred thousand francs, ten minutes before attempting the holdup of our lives, what would have happened? For a second the room just stopped dead. Most of the people were onlookers and cops, they knew we were replaying the scene and knew I'd be leaving without anything, but it made no difference, a feeling of terror settled over everyone. Even I thought for an instant that I'd really won that money. The judge's eyes met mine and we stared at each other for a good few seconds. Then he snapped out of it, asked the croupier to throw the ball again. Marin's face passed before me, I imagined his satisfied smile, the wink he'd have given me, then I shook my head gently and placed my bet again, still the 36 because, I told myself, it won't come up twice. Slowly I placed the pile of chips on the table, looked intently at the croupier without knowing what expression I wore on my face, and I waited. I think it's the 15 that came up. The 36 was still going through my head and would stay there for a while yet, but I'd lost my twenty-five thousand francs.

Next there was the disturbance. It was the classic scene: my wife and I had just lost fifty thousand francs, so I had to stand up and raise my voice, saying that this was unacceptable, I'd never seen such a thing in a gambling establishment, not anywhere else, not in Los Angeles, not in Tokyo, it was an insult, no way to handle a client, I'd never been treated like that before, no one had ever dealt that way with Sir Oliver Danforth.

That was the name we'd decided on, Andrei, Marin, and I: Oliver Danforth. It had to be a credible name, and we'd needed one that suggested a man both rich and high-strung, also it had to fit me, fit my physical appearance, plus be of English background, to be more chic. We'd hesitated over several, I still remember: Francis Good, Lawrence Brandywine, Philip Damon, and in the end we chose Oliver Danforth.

So I would fuss and fume in the name of Oliver Danforth, without getting pale, without letting my voice quaver, without tensing up, I would go through the paces of the offended rich man who has come to have a good time in this establishment and who will not be duped, a man who thought he was in an honest house, Call the director, this is a scandal, *Monsieur le directeur,* I had one hundred thousand francs right here in my attaché case, I wager fifty of it, I lose, I bend down to take out the other fifty, I reach into my attaché case, and what do I find, well quite simply, *Monsieur le directeur,* I find they aren't there anymore, in an establishment like yours, excuse me, I have never seen the like anywhere, to be robbed in the street, on a bench, in a park, yes, but not here, excuse me, not here, fifty thousand francs, *Monsieur le directeur.*

The object of the game, therefore, was to have him invite me to settle the matter in private, in his office, which is what happened on the real evening, with the real director, and what an actor hired for the reconstruction was trying to imitate: the embarrassment, the ballet of head movements, the plastered-down hair, the white suit, the polished shoes, but he wasn't believable. I told the judge how the truth was eluding us, because of the actor, that he would try his best, of course, but you couldn't believe in him. I had to explain to the judge the impasse we were risking by replaying the scene, that it was a game of strategy, of glances, of minute interior details, like delicate clockwork, if you prefer, I told the judge. You must understand: you've just lost fifty thousand francs at roulette, as if by chance at that moment you start a scene and you announce to the director of a casino that you've been robbed, well let me tell you, *Monsieur le juge,* that the director of such an establishment does not believe you for one second, and let me tell you also that I knew he didn't believe me. I pretended to be outraged, and he pretended to be embarrassed. That's how we found ourselves in his office, both of us knowing for a fact that there wasn't a shred of truth in all this, but both of us forced to play out our respective roles.

We went through the scene in the office anyway, because that's why we were there, the judge reminded me, to reconstruct the events. The director and I went upstairs, followed by the judge, then the photographer, then the three policemen con-

stantly shadowing me. Instead of a rear wall, the office had a large
inclined window through which you could see the entire gaming
room, as if from a command center, or rather, from an airport control tower, because of the tilted glass, and just as you might have
seen men busy out on runways you could follow the constant activity of the gamblers, croupiers, machines. From the gaming
room, however, you couldn't see anything of the director's dimly
lit office, because seen from below, the window was a giant mirror
reflecting the crooked moves of cheats. Thus the glass did double
duty: the director spent his evenings watching from behind the
window, and the supervisors spent theirs studying the mirror.
We'd watched films on that, about surveillance systems in casinos,
in banks, in every place where money acts as a magnet, and in casinos there is always someone who sees everything, and that man
who sees everything must watch the room supervisors, while
they, the room supervisors, must watch the croupiers, and the
croupiers, meanwhile, watch the clients. It's quite a massive pyra-
mid, and that's why we, for our part, had decided to go directly
from the bottom to the top floor, from the client to the director,
without any middlemen. That's why I'd had to shout, Get me the
director!

The director waved me to a seat in his deluxe lookout tur-
ret and he smiled, I mean, the actor smiled, which the real director had never done. He didn't smile like that, I told the judge, the
director took me seriously right down the line, and drove me to
cross the line, in fact, precisely without any smiles or courtesy. In
reality, the director had sat down in his big upholstered swivel
chair as though at the controls of a space shuttle and had turned

his back on me to look out at the room. I'd kept making my scene, complaining politely and with class. Then he swung his chair halfway around, formed a triangle with his hands by placing his fingertips together, like this, and stared at me sternly, wearily, and he said something like, Monsieur, I've never seen you here and I'm not in the habit of wasting my time, but he'd just barely gotten started when I pulled the gun from under my belt and pointed it at him. They supplied me with everything I asked for: a white silk scarf, cigars, a new suit, money, a piece: if I'd asked for a makeup girl, they'd have brought me one on a platter. When you're the accused, I thought, you're the king and ringmaster, because they can't do anything without you. Then I asked the director not to move, telling him that the slightest movement would prove fatal for him, and that he should not try to alert anyone because there were many of us, all heavily armed. It was partly true: that there were many of us, no, but heavily armed, yes, Marin especially, an arsenal in his pockets, we'd joked the day before, smoke grenades hooked to the lining of his jacket, knives at his belt, and the revolver fully loaded. At that precise moment he was to have reached the third floor, posted himself by the elevator, and I was to take the director there, after which we'd proceed to the count room. So I went behind the desk, I shoved the gun barrel in the director's back, right by his spine to make the point, and we went out into the hall. Not a word, only silence all around, and the metal gun barrel held against his jacket, directing his body. There was no one in the fluorescent light of the hall, no one anywhere to interrupt the sequence of events, it was almost strange, to imagine that it was so easy, so like what we'd envisioned for months as the best-case scenario, the perfect operation, meaning the one that doesn't happen, the one you quickly dismiss, figuring on this or that obstacle, screwup, mistake, and now, on the contrary, it was happening. I was aware of the judge still behind me observing my gestures, my tics, the muscles of my cheek that might be twitching, and I felt like telling him it was useless, that this time was just for laughs. Because he'd said, the judge, that he had to decide on documentary evidence, he'd said, I want to learn what kind of man you are. We crowded into the elevator—the director, the revolver, the judge, the photographer; with one hand I pushed button 3, with the other I kept the gun glued to my hostage, then the steel doors closed. I saw my face in a mirror, the tuxedo still clean and the shirt still white, I saw my eyes worrying about myself, wondering confusedly what I was doing there on the thirty-first when I should have been eating and drinking in a fine restaurant like everyone else, throwing flowers from my balcony, plenty of champagne on the table, the sort of thoughts you sometimes have in limbo or between two floors, so I didn't see why I shouldn't be doing like everybody else, I didn't see why I shouldn't have my New Year's Eve too, my private party, and I don't know, yes, fast as that, when the door was about to open, I don't know, perhaps the director said something like Go fuck yourself, because maybe I'd said Nice evening for a New Year's celebration, anyway at that moment I definitely cracked, at that moment something broke inside of me, at that moment I felt the trigger loose under my finger, I didn't shoot, but I felt it. All the same I did hit him in the face, my free arm struck his jaw on account of that "Go fuck your-self." To say today whether he used the familiar *tu* with me, or whether habit or fear had made him polite, I don't know any-more, but I do know that he felt that slap like a storm blowing through his skull, and a trickle of blood showed in the mirror, be-cause you don't insult people like that, I told him, even enemies, even strangers. I tried to go gently the day of the reconstruction, with the actor, but when he muttered his own "Go fuck yourself," I swear, the blow went off almost as hard, his head hitting the mir-ror, seeing himself bleed, Sorry, I told him, but it was already too late. The judge gloated off in his corner, then the doors opened, it seemed to me we'd gone all the way to the top of a tall building, but we'd actually gone up one floor.

As planned Marin was waiting for me on the third floor, leaning against a wall with the cool composure of a movie star. As planned there was a cop, who'd dressed up as Marin and thought glowering would make him look the part. I thought, Lose the chewing gum if you want any chance of measuring up to his ankle. With the tired director in front, Marin beside me keeping an eye on him, gun in hand, we'd proceeded to the count room, the door at the end of the long hall and growing larger with our approach, Count Room written in front of us on a white back-ground, locked door, code, Open it you bastard, muttered Marin between his teeth to the director, who was weakening, or losing heart, or beginning to realize that basically, whatever he did, he wouldn't get out alive. But that wasn't true, in our plans it was clearly stated that we wouldn't kill. We had never in all that time we spent setting things up, never even mentioned shedding blood, because it was to be, we kept saying, the absolute perfection of crime. So the director, he would have to have wanted it from the depths of his soul, death, have to have imagined the scene a hundred times in his office, the theoretical day of an always possible holdup on the premises, he would have to have written his death himself, I would tell the judge, to have spoken to us like that. Head down, panting, unsteady on his feet, he finally lifted his hand to the code pad on the wall, trembling, hesitant, even his hand was sweating so hard we couldn't tell which act he was putting on, frightened or reluctant, still holding back from punching in that fucking code, Hurry up asshole, the 4, the 2, the 1, the 3, the 6, tapping a whole bunch of numbers, maybe fifteen twenty, Marin and I even wondered if it was some kind of a joke, this combination, if maybe slugging him wouldn't speed things up. But the heavy door swung open onto darkness, and then there was light in the room, on the safes, our eyes immediately drawn to the two armored cubes facing us like two Frigidaires from the 1950s but which to us, at that moment, seemed more like Egyptian tombs, since we pictured them full to the brim, more than we'd hoped for, and the end of a long hard road. The director appeared to get a grip on himself, took an almost confident tone, as though suddenly he had simply condescended to bring us there, and said, The alarm system is quite sophisticated, as if he were giving us a demonstration, if you get within three feet, a siren goes off, and Marin smiled at him, broadly enough for him to stop talking, to understand that for us everything was going as planned. I thought at that point we were going to lose him, a fit or a sudden panic, that he'd collapse in front of us, at that point I understood that the worst threat for men like him, it wasn't death and what would happen to them throughout eternity, it was to see their evening go to hell right in front of their eyes. And when he realized that we'd taken care of his whole alarm system, that we were real professionals, he said, Son of a bitch, he said, Son of a bitch, said it twice, but he shouldn't have, and those words in my mind took off once, twice, like a tornado inside, so the last word when I was sure I'd heard right, when I asked Did I hear you right? and then shouted Did I hear you right? well the word "bitch" coincided with the muffled sound of a blow to his head, the word "bitch" went pow in my face right on my nerves and his face bled a little more. I banged his head a few times against a safe and he went down. Like an echo from behind there was Marin, who'd said "No," but too late, I lashed out, I almost killed him, that's for sure, but it was an accident, and that's why he didn't die, because if I'd really tried to kill him, I told the judge, I would obviously have succeeded, because after all, I concluded, I'm a professional.

The judge thanked me, and he said, I think that will be enough. Because he, the judge, wasn't interested in the rest, or rather the rest, he already knew that. The judge, what he wanted, he said, was to learn what kind of man I was, meaning what my failings were, so he'd know how lenient to be. The judge, when you get right down to it, never understood a thing about this whole business.

There was no one outside anymore. In the police van, I caught another look at a cop's watch: it was 10:50. Then, I remember, I cried a lot.

3

It didn't take us long to empty the safes, maybe ten minutes to fill the bag with packets of brand-new bills, and we stashed the director where the money had been. He'll bounce back in no time, I told Marin, he's a bit done in, that's all. I'll skip details about the blood getting everywhere and the trouble we had shutting the door on the tired body, but he finally went in. I had blood on my shirt and had to button my jacket to hide it. Then with a wink Marin and I separated out on the landing.

I went back downstairs to Jeanne in her white dress. We played roulette one last time so as to appear at ease before walking out the front door. We lost one last time as though it were nothing, then nodded politely to the bouncers and swept down the steps like royalty. Meanwhile Marin had climbed the service stairs to the roof, as planned. Carrying the canvas bag stuffed with five million francs, practically jumping out of his skin if a lightbulb so much as sputtered, he went up the three floors, opened the boiler room with a passkey, and went out on the roof. I reflected that I could have killed him in the count room and parked him in the second safe with his share of the take soaked in his own blood. I reflected that deep down, that's what he would have liked, this man I pictured lying on the roof watching his cigarette ash burn down, waiting. The parking valet brought us the Mercedes, then we shot onto the highway, the sea gleamed beneath the harbor lights, and heading for the harbor we did not exceed the speed limit. Can you imagine, I told Jeanne, getting busted for speeding, that would be worse than Al Capone. She choked laughing, she was like that, basically she couldn't have cared less about what would happen. On the roof, Marin must already have given the signal to Lucho with the flashlight. That roof, it was like a luxurious terrace above the beach. We'd remarked on that several times while watching Andrei's film, that they should have made a summer bar out of it, a nighttime solarium, a cool, refreshing spot for their clientele. You mean a lunarium, Andrei had said.

Lucho had climbed up onto a roof as well, on top of the apartment building he'd selected from which to fly his balloon by remote control. And here's what Lucho had to do: wait on his roof for Marin's light signal, send the balloon to the casino roof, let Marin put the money into the gondola, get the whole thing airborne again, and guide it out to sea, to be retrieved by the boat, after which he would rejoin us, when we all met again a little later at our rendezvous in the warehouse for the big scene of the division of the loot. That's all he had to do, Lucho, nothing else.

We'd had long discussions about our respective roles, to decide who would row the boat out there, after I'd made it clear that strutting around the roulette table was enough for me, thank you. But you'll be the first one there, Marin had said, and believe me, he'd added, I'd rather be out on the water than scrambling down a roof surrounded by security guards. I'd suggested we find a different solution, all we had to do was bring the balloon back near the warehouse, on dry land. Too dangerous, said Lucho, too chancy, no, the best and coolest spot was the sea. So how many times had I seen myself out there, in a boat in the middle of the roadstead, a dark silhouette in the dark, and how many times imagined what easy prey I'd make if things went wrong, and felt the barrage of bullets ripping into my back, my body falling, tipping, and plunging bloodied into the sea. How many times that evening had I thought about retreating, speeding off with Jeanne and the Mercedes down the highway, popping in a tape, blasting music from the speakers, a complete contrast with the lapping of the boat moving through the water and the erratic creaking of the oarlocks.

The boat was hidden on the water, in the shadow of a freighter, three hundred yards from the warehouse. Just to be nice, I suppose, Jeanne went down with me to the dock and untied the boat without a word. She didn't say anything either when I kissed her, thanked her for everything, and hugged her as though I would never see her again. I jumped into the skiff and I rowed, slowly at first, watching Jeanne's pale form, the black mass of the freighter dwindling in the distance, then I rowed faster. The few lights that still showed at that hour, the silent wind skimming over the smooth surface, everything was driving me out to dark water, where the streetlights, Lucho had said, would give up before we did. I felt drawn by an invisible magnet, and terra firma, the world of the living—it all seemed for an instant to have vanished forever. You could still see the bridge in the night, its piers planted in the water, and hear the hum of the distant cars blending with the splashing of the oars. Soon it would be midnight. This, I thought, is where I should have brought a bottle of champagne, just for me under the moonless sky, to wish myself a Happy New Year. Then I signaled Lucho with my flashlight, and I waited in darkness for the little balloon to appear, coming toward me, growing larger as I watched, landing, if all went well, in the boat. There was silence, too. Suddenly in the gloom I could make out the cloth globe of the balloon, the hot breath of the gas keeping it inflated and floating through the calm air. The five million francs wafted on the wind, so light that night over the sea, and I thought, if we humans could figure out how to weigh so little, many of us would surely do something else with our lives. That's what I thought, gazing at the heavens, and I stood up in the boat. I unshipped the oars, it was like a child's dream, and the balloon came closer, I prayed it wouldn't veer off, that it would keep coming, to me, until I could take it in my arms, like a child's plaything.

But at that moment, just when I'd forgotten everything else, even my fear, at that moment I heard a sound like gunfire, coming from the harbor, bursts in all directions, I looked around wildly but could see nothing, I was panting and yelling, I lay down in the boat, covered my head with my hands, heart straining and pumping like mad, now I couldn't see anything but the wet bottom of the boat, but I heard, like bullets whistling in the night, muffled noises, I considered shouting, saying that I surrendered, but they wouldn't have heard me, so I raised my head to take another look, and I saw in the distance on the sea, I saw a blue light rising into the sky, then a red light, a green one, another blue one and clusters exploding way up high. Then I took a huge breath: it was midnight. And I told myself, well, Uncle and Marin, they thought they were so clever, why didn't they think of this on a New Year's Eve. On the bridge, cars began to honk, ever more vivid lights reached out across the water, and uproar enveloped the sea. The balloon was just overhead, fifteen feet above the boat, I grasped the cord hanging from the gondola, pulled on it to shut down the device, then the hot breath was stilled, the bag softly deflated, and with the sound of fabric flapping in the wind, the gondola landed gently before me, in the boat. I drew the sack of money from its basket, to make sure I wasn't dreaming. And then I thought, for the memory of a bag full of money in the middle of the sea, I'd be forever happy they'd sent me there, alone on the placid water. But out there I had nothing more to do, neither think nor dream, only row toward the harbor, steering clear of the lights.

I threw the mooring line onto the dock; Marin and Lucho were waiting there, and both dashed to grab the rope. Then, still standing in the boat, I put one foot up on the asphalt and casually tossed out the money, as if I'd been holding a case of sardines. Be careful, hissed Marin, who would have liked to speak louder but didn't dare. He did give me his hand to help me out of the boat, though. Lucho had retrieved his balloon, and none of us said anything, walking to the warehouse, until the door rumbled shut behind us. Inside, bathed in the yellowish light, you'd have thought it was three hours earlier: the five of us sat instinctively in the same chairs, slumping in the same positions, our guns lying in front of us again, as if nothing had happened, as if the money sitting impressively on the table in its bulging sack were no different from the cognac bottle. And it was the same, same silence, same weariness, same waiting. We'd brought the whole thing off and it was as though we hadn't realized that. The creased fabric of the bag only hinted at the money it contained; there might just as well have been dirty clothes or yesterday's newspapers folded up inside, we'd never have known. I stared at the bag a long time thinking about that, the idea that we'd filled it ourselves, that bag, yet I was still managing to doubt its contents. But Marin took hold of it by the bottom with both hands and emptied it over the table, and I stopped thinking like an idiot, and the money spread out in front of us, thick bundles piled one atop the other, overlapping, sliding down the mountain gradually heaped up by the accumulation of small bills and slowly taking over the whole table. No question, there were definitely lots of bundles.

We sat there for quite a while, without moving, without touching the money, with only the peaceful rhythm of our breathing floating in the gray air. Five million is easier to divide by five than by four said Andrei, and nudged Marin, who at that moment didn't notice friend Andrei's laughing and friendly expression. Not once, I thought, not once have we mentioned what we'd do with this money, or the dreams we each had, a million serious francs that would have inspired the most fantastic visions in other people and merely gave us the vague feeling, the obscure presentiment that somewhere a future ought to exist. One day I'd told Andrei that with the money, I would finally quit, and take off. But where to, he'd asked me, without even expecting a reply, his question so obviously drawing a blank, it's true, where to. Even when the idea of a trip, train, plane had often crossed my mind, not once had I been able to glimpse a destination, the color of a city, or its name, only the gray-and-green sweep of a railway landscape, or the sun peeking above some clouds, only a circular trajectory at unspecified speed, but where to? So with our shining eyes and cautious smiles, that evening, we saw nothing but the solid heap of bills instead of even the slightest fantasy or new day or dream fulfilled. It was already written—Marin's silhouette in front of his bay window, the sodden nights at the Lord Jim, and the jaunts in the Mercedes to the north of the city to go see Auntie on Saturdays. Already written, the future history of the "family," and soon the only thing missing, when talking about Marin, would be calling him "Uncle." Something else I caught sight of that same night: the image of Jeanne as an old Auntie.

We counted the money and divided it by five, in neatly stacked piles shoved in front of each of us. I looked at Lucho and said, We could play poker now. But he shook his head no, and he didn't feel like laughing. I told him to lighten up a bit, that every-

thing was going great, and I made a point of adding, with a side-
long glance at Marin, I remember adding, At least you, Lucho,
you can feel free because you aren't a complete member of the
family. But Marin, he acted as if he hadn't heard, continuing to
fiddle with his share, riffling the packets loosely with his thumb.
Okay, he said, let's go. We each put the money away in attaché
cases we opened on the table, then closed simultaneously, all five,
with a crisp slam. We retrieved our revolvers and headed pur-
posefully for the exit, carrying our cases in one hand. For my
part, I was clearly going to be saying good-bye to them. Outside,
however, Marin walked toward the Mercedes with Jeanne,
walked away from us in the shadow of the warehouse, calling
back in a normal voice through the cold night air, See you tomorrow.

He said "See you tomorrow." So perhaps I almost lost it.
Perhaps I came close to leaving them my share and just tearing
off into the darkness. Perhaps everything became suddenly
cloudy and speeded up and drowned all at once inside of me.
Perhaps that's what I should have done, abruptly said good-bye
to them and run away. But I didn't have enough time, they didn't
either, no one had time to do anything, either to embrace or
whatever, when Marin pulled the door up on its tracks, heaved it
wide open, when the five of us found ourselves outside, and
walking off, the only thing for us to do was put our hands up.

We hadn't heard a thing from inside, not one of us, even
opening the door we didn't see any suspicious lights. They'd
turned off their headlights and cut their engines back at the main

road, they'd sneaked up like foxes. They swooped out of the dark shouting, Police, don't move! Then all the glare and the rotating blue gizmos, us dazzled by their powerful lights, them protected behind their cars blocking off the road, doors open to act as shields, the cops in cowboy-position we figured—legs spread, arms straight out front, revolvers aimed at our hearts—but with all that light in our eyes we couldn't see too well. They kept us at a distance like that for a few seconds, not knowing themselves what moves or attitudes to adopt. But now we, all five of us lit up from the front, we could see one another just fine. I looked over at Marin, then Lucho, then Andrei, one by one, all of them, meeting their eyes in succession. If we'd only had time to pull them, our revolvers, we wouldn't have turned them against the cops, but against one another, because we were already hunting for the guilty man in someone else's face. The guilty man, though, it was crystal clear already, clear that the weakest one of us had cracked, at the last moment maybe but cracked clean through, and I imagined him, Lucho, up on his building, guiding the balloon toward the water, I imagined him already knowing what we'd find waiting for us when we left. You shouldn't have had those drinks, Lucho. But in my panic I didn't work all that out, instead there was emptiness, and suspicion hanging like a guillotine blade over everyone's head. And I pictured this scene: Marin pointing his gun at me, me pointing mine at Lucho, Lucho aiming at Andrei, and Andrei ready to shoot Marin. We'd have left Jeanne out of the whole thing. If I could have, I'd have taken her by the hand and we'd have run through a hail of bullets, and I would have protected her from the madness of men. But the lot of us, standing quietly with our hands in the air, all we could do from now on was take orders from a police lieutenant. Throw down your weapons, he said, turn around, hands against the wall.

We should have obeyed immediately, tossed away our weapons, they would have slid along the pavement toward the cops. But we kept looking at one another, and Marin was staring at us, with a distant or vacant expression, and he slowly closed his eyes, then opened them. We reached inside our belts, the gun butts against our bare skin, hands moving cautiously, our faces soaking up the glare from the lights, still glancing discreetly at one another to figure out what to do, and our movements seemed to take forever. We were all four like machines, acting frame by frame. We still clutched our attaché cases in one hand, and with the other were drawing out our revolvers, they were visible now, all we had to do was throw them in front of us, and the cops facing us were still silent, with a silence that was expanding, growing huge in my brain, but I was going to do it, toss the revolver into the light, Andrei was going to do it, our arms were already in position, our movements had almost ceased, our heads were bent, and there was Marin, his slow wink again, there was his arm moving out, shoulder-high, his index finger gently hugging the trigger, and we saw, we understood, we did not give up our guns. We stretched our arms out in front of us, barely looked, more like sensed we'd be acting together, sprang into the shadows and fired, one shot, two, three, diving symmetrically,

Andrei and I to one side, Marin to the other, he'd carried Jeanne along in his fall, we were hanging in the air, still firing, now the target of enemy bullets crashing into the metal siding of the warehouse, the lights whirling and seeking us along the wall, we landed and rolled along the ground, stretched out, still protected by our motion, the fusillade increasing in all directions. Lucho was still on his feet, in the center of the action, hands in the air, his revolver on the ground, he wasn't moving, just shaking, paralyzed by the shattering din of the bullets all around. Why didn't he jump, that idiot, why did he stay there sticking up like a cross, as if he were waiting for it to happen, waiting to get blown away, us screaming at him, telling him to get down, but he was as if dead to the world, standing right in the light, or he really wanted to die. At that moment, if I'd had to, I would still have saved him. We'd have tried to get away, but the cops were machine-gunning, it was almost impossible even to move now. I saw the C15 a few yards away, we would have needed to make it there and slide underneath it, out of reach of the lights, but it was so far away. Andrei got halfway to his feet to get a better aim, raised his revolver in front of his eyes, stood up, I told him to get down but he stayed standing, shooting straight, torso erect, with the floodlight, the halogen circle flitting impatiently through the emptiness, like a spotlight seeking an actor on the stage, I told him to get down, I said "Duck" or "Watch out" or "Hide, Andrei" because that spotlight, that spot was like the lightning before the thunder, and when it's on you it's gunfire that comes next, and that's just what happened, Get down Andrei, shit, get down fast, but they'd already opened up, already gotten him in their sights, and Andrei got down of course, he lay down of course, but crumpled, shrieking, blood splattering around, his mouth spitting that same red color pouring from his belly, the bullet deep in his abdomen, dead center. And I shouted Andrei's name, for a long time, I screamed, already in tears, my voice ragged, echoing over the asphalt, and I added Bastards, stretching it out, loud, Bastards I shouted like a grenade hurled from my throat. He didn't drop his revolver, Andrei, he held his stomach with his left hand, and with his right, as his head lay on the ground, he kept firing without seeing anymore what or whom he was aiming at, but he hit the cops' floodlight, it sputtered a fraction of a second and went out, his arm fell, it was completely dark. All firing stopped. It was quiet.

How many seconds then went by without any sign of life from either side, not even the wind stirring the air. Then they turned on their flashlights, the white beams began slicing the night, and I realized at that point, I realized it was all over. I heard Andrei's tortured breathing, their heavy steps as they came closer. And I also realized, in that same silence of the grave, that now there were only two of us, Andrei and I, in the cops' net. Marin and Jeanne were no longer there, behind us. They'd managed to slip away sometime before. I don't believe I was even surprised. I raised my hands and announced that I wasn't armed anymore, which was true; they came closer, frisked me, then took my hands and cuffed me without a word. I heard the click of a lighter, I turned my head, I saw Lucho's face in the glow of the flame, lighting a cigarette. And I don't think I was surprised, either, to see him shake hands with the cops and heave a great sigh of relief. And I can say, Lucho, at this point in time, I can say: I knew you'd crack. I didn't know when, but I knew. In the end, though, even that day, at that moment, it wasn't you I was really thinking of.

I remember looking at my shoes. They'd gotten a little wet, and my feet, uncomfortably damp, were fidgeting inside the muddy leather. A thousand francs, they'd cost. Then I looked up at the cops in their kepis in front of me, their torsos rocking back and forth in unison with the jouncing of the van on the uneven pavement, and the headlights behind them shining on the bars, the beams wavering as well, depending on whether we were driving fast, braking, speeding up. On the highway, between the stony faces of the two cops, through the window at the back of their heads, I remember seeing slowly pass by, clearly visible, the six huge red letters of the word CASINO.

Part Three

....

I

When my cell door swung open that day in March, I hoisted my duffel bag to my shoulder and followed the guard through the corridors and gates. They handed back the precise contents of my pockets seven years earlier: three used bus tickets, my beat-up wallet, and the keys to the old C15. But the old C15 had long since left the land of living objects. Then I crossed the courtyard, passed through another gate, and yet another one, and when the guard opened the small door set in the main entrance gate, he nodded to me. I turned around one last time, looking up at the facade; there was the French flag waving in the sunshine, and above that I saw the window of my cell. I thought I saw my hands still gripping the bars.

All you had to do was pull the chair over to the wall, step up on it, and look out. The bars didn't matter, you could see a long way off. Nothing else counted there except seeing a long way off, the surrounding area with its maritime atmosphere, the land forever rushing into the water. The rocks, the granite, the jutting coastline, the sand, everything advances, withdraws, wears away, and as you imagine each step on the farthest reach of the shore, the farthest point will always remain one step away. But from many places, for the person looking out, from many of the prison windows, the sun doesn't sink behind the horizon but disappears into a corner or behind a building, because the city cuts off the distant sea. And in the city itself, you quickly forget that shadowy marine presence, you focus more easily on the grid pattern of the straight streets, so heedless of the blustery winds, the arsenal in decline with its long walls still keeping up a good front, the rusty harbor, and the surrounding countryside, so green that the damp gray roofs look that much taller. No basilica, or great central square, or half-timbered houses, or beneficent fountain in that city, but neon signs, wind, a railroad station, a bridge across the sea, a prison. People don't come here, they just pass through. Or they're already here.

I looked out the window three thousand four hundred times. I spent two thousand five hundred afternoons on my flimsy mattress staring at the cracks in the ceiling. I took one thousand seven hundred walks in the concrete courtyard to fight off cramps, stiff muscles. I popped pills nine hundred times to avoid seeing you, Marin, or your smile in my dreams. I worked. I bent pieces of iron and folded cardboard boxes in the basement workshops. I put together meals for trains and planes. In all those years, I packaged five hundred thousand food trays without ever knowing where the plane would land. I often thought about you, Marin. Where would you go, to New York, perhaps, or South America? I often thought about you, Marin, I swear. I thought about the food tray traveling along the conveyor belt, its trip in a refrigerated truck, and then the airport, straight onto the plane, and I thought about the flight attendant handing them out, those trays, with you in first class, smiling at that woman in that plane, then unwrapping and eating that food I'd packaged for you, Marin. I swear to you I spat in each tray, and I knew that one day you'd feel my spit in your mouth.

You, the briefcase full of money in the baggage hold . . . no, not in the hold, because you would have insisted on keeping it with you in spite of its weight, too precious to check with the other luggage, you, you wouldn't have wanted to see the brief-case fall onto the runway, slam open on impact with bills flying everywhere on the warm breath of the jet engines. You were often afraid of many things, Marin.

It's my turn now, my turn to tell you about my life, the tepid chicory in the chipped cups, the light turned on every two hours at night to make sure no one has committed suicide, the triangular steps in the courtyard, and the TV programs picked by three cons voting in one cell. I would have watched less of it, television, if you'd been with me, sprawled right on the floor and smoking your huge cigars. With two of us, we could have bought ourselves some cognac to make the evenings go faster. But you know about it, all of it, the first days when you just can't swallow a thing, when smoking with all that bile mixed in would have burned out your bronchi, you can't bring yourself to turn on the TV, or read a newspaper in the morning, and the shame of sitting on the plank seat of the toilet, your cellmates so taciturn from sleeping pills, and some weeks that drag on worse than others. But you didn't come, Marin, neither prisoner, nor visitor, you forgot your "family." It's always been too late, Marin, too late to explain why you ran away, so don't try for any reconciliation. Don't try to revive that old homey feeling, from when you talked nonstop in front of your bay window as if to make us believe there was nothing between us and the casino safes but clear glass. I'm surprised you didn't frame your ideas and hang them on the wall, but that's all over now and I'm thinking of you, I swear, I'm thinking of you, Marin.

When my cell door swung open that day in March, I walked down the avenue lined with plane trees to the intersection, and I waited inside the bus shelter for number 72 to brake to a halt at a wave of my hand. On the outside, I thought, just by snapping your fingers you can stop a crowded bus. I found a seat facing an old lady; she looked away because of my staring at her, I mean because of my forgetting that you're not supposed to watch people like that. So I observed the city streaming by outside, the new stores opened there, the new cars I'd seen on TV, the new Mercedes models, and the trim new look in men's clothing. The sun was shining all over the sidewalks, on the shop windows, into the bus, and I saw my poorly shaved face reflected in the glass, floating over everything, I saw how the streets were older and my hair badly cut, I saw my tired, sunless skin, and I did the figures in my head, wondering: For dogs you multiply by seven but for years in stir, it's by how much?

2

The old lady facing me, she reminded me of Auntie. Auntie, also facing me, in the visiting room. She came to see me, once, one single time to salvage her pride or the family or Marin. In spite of her age, she had gone through the exhausting procedure to obtain a visitor's pass, and the number 72 bus had dropped her off at the end of the avenue, all dressed in black, barely two months after Uncle's death. Every day of her life she must have seen that prison as a threat, a black cloud, a ball and chain on all our actions, the prison that had laid claim for a century to the only high ground in the city—120 feet above sea level—and was visible from every part of it. Even from the cemetery you could see it. As for us, the 250 inmates, we called it the Belvedere. We could see trains rolling by below, heading inland, and for seven years even inland looked good to me. She sat down in the visiting room facing me, looking behind her, around her, as if worried someone would catch her there, as if Uncle himself, with his stooped body, now turning to dust, were still weighing on her, on that glass cage that confined us for thirty minutes.

Andrei is dead, she said. She told me how they'd taken him to the hospital, how he'd died in the ambulance, how she'd seen to having him buried. I went to the morgue, she said. She was crying a little. I asked to see the body, she said. She assured the morgue employees that she could pay, she'd take care of everything, the coffin, the priest, and they finally said okay.

After that, she talked about Marin. The police looked everywhere for him, she told me, but without success, they say they haven't any proof against him, she told me, they can't do a thing. So I asked her if she knew where he was, and she didn't answer. I said coldly: He left without me, with the money. She took a deep breath and explained that he'd left town the day after the disaster, with Jeanne, and that they expected to return soon, after things had settled down. He left without me, with the money. That he wanted to start a new life, come back without any problems, that we'd forget everything, but I interrupted her, I pounded my fist on the wall: He took off with the money and without me, you got that, he cut and ran without me. She shook her head no, it had all happened so fast, and she begged me, crying harder: It's not Marin's fault, I swear, you can come see him when you get out, he'll help you, I swear it, even if I'm dead, she said, he'll help you.

She'd been dead a long time in fact by that day in March, and there weren't even any flowers on the common grave, the marble slab with their names on it together from now on, Andrei, Uncle, and Auntie in that sloping cemetery in the southern part of the city, that plot, once so well maintained, serving as a rallying point, or a real family home. And in front of the tomb I thought things over, for seven years I'd thought things over but standing there with the dead I thought things over some more, because I thought there were two names missing on the marble,

I thought they weren't in the ground, Marin and Lucho, neither one of them, because both of them had been there to fuck things up. I'm not saying that you knew it was going to go wrong, Marin, I'm not saying that. I'm saying: You went that far, Marin, you even abandoned your family.

I left the cemetery and I walked. I walked along the highway. I passed in front of the casino. I sat on a bench in a park. I would have chatted with anyone at all, actually, about what I was going to do. I looked at my shoes, worn out from not being worn, I looked at the fountain spitting fitfully into the dry air, and I waited. I can't say now whether it was the night or the silence or what, but I had to wait there, surrounded by privet bushes and cypresses. I saw the harbor still rusting away, the cylindrical smokestacks, the sheet-metal cubes, I saw the edge of the sea between the sailboat masts.

When you get out of prison, doctors say, you shouldn't walk too much, because of weakness and flabby muscles. I stayed in limbo for an hour, on that bench, running my hands over the folds in my coat, watching the birds in a circle on the gravel. It still gets dark early in March, so I stood up and I went across the park, the streets, the main avenue, past shops closing up, along sidewalks, through thinning crowds of people, into the first brasserie I came to, and I ordered a beer. I asked the waiter for a phone book. My finger ran down the lists of names, I tore a slip of paper and on it I wrote an address and a first name: Luciano. I thought, A long time ago now, we called him Lucho. I also thought: Are guys really so stupid they don't even leave town, or do they really think that *I'm* that stupid?

3

But first, I went back to the Lord Jim. That wasn't its name anymore. They must have changed it because of some problems, said the bartender, who was new as well. Now the bar was called the Billy Budd. That night I rang the buzzer around midnight, and I looked straight into the camera over the entrance. When the door opened and I walked in I found that little if anything had changed. Elbows firmly planted on the bar, a cognac please. And what did seem strange to me in there was not knowing the bartender's name.

So I wondered what I was doing there, near the mauve couches, standing at the very same bar, and waiting for something like a shadow to come up behind me, tap me on the shoulder, a shadow that would want us to be brothers again. But of course there was no one, you weren't there anymore, Marin, drinking at the bar. And your absence at that moment, the empty barstool to my right, it was as if I'd had a pebble in my shoe, you follow me, a pebble that was keeping me from walking or sitting down, something between me and myself, certainly, but sometimes pebbles like that are hard to carry around, I felt as though it were shooting through my bloodstream, up to my heart or my brain, and I couldn't get it out. As long as you're alive, Marin, I'll always have a pebble in my shoe.

He wouldn't have flinched. If I'd been able to tell him that, between two cognacs, he wouldn't even have blinked, because you understand everything, I thought, you've always understood everything quickly, Marin. And we could have fallen into each other's arms, killed a bottle talking over old times and old jobs, gone out to fight in front of the entrance, and I'd have laid you out on the pavement, kicked you in the jaw, and told you we were through, that you had no more business here on this earth.

But the taste of cognac, in that club, even the odor, almost, it made me feel sick. And the loneliness as well. You know you're going downhill, I thought, when you start staring at a glass instead of drinking up. So outside, in the light of the streetlamps, I headed into the wind. Aimless wandering, I thought, I'll have plenty of time for that from now on. Time to admire the sea under the arches of the old bridge. Time to study stones between two cigarettes. The pathetic seagulls circling over the dunes. Tired boulders that still seem to think it's worth it.

I ran through the faces in my head, Andrei's, pale and bloodless; Uncle's, on his bed; Luciano's, in the flashlight beams of the cops, lighting his cigarette; Jeanne's, finally, Jeanne, in her white dress, and I thought that already she was the only one left.

She, Jeanne, living alone now in a one-bedroom apartment on the outskirts of town, her face drawn with solitude and weariness, when I rang downstairs and saw her lean over her balcony on the fourth or fifth floor, for a second I felt I should sim-

ply go away. I went upstairs anyhow, she opened her door to me
anyhow, but she had lost her smile. She went looking for it deep
down, her smile, and she put one on her face to welcome me.
She let me kiss her, for appearances, and let me in, but that was
for appearances too. She'd opened her door before I reached her
floor, and she hadn't stayed waiting at the threshold for me. I
knocked automatically, pushing the door open at the same time,
and only then did she greet me, only then did I kiss her, Jeanne,
her skin still cool, her cheeks a little gaunt, small circles under
her eyes, because she'd grown older, after all. We sat down facing
each other on the creaking springs of the armchairs and I said
dumb things, stuff like "I'm free now" or "That's it, it's over" and
"I'm going to start a new life." I looked around the living room,
the front hall, for some sign of a connection to us, to me, to
Marin, a knickknack or something, an expression on her face,
but I didn't find a thing. Even her eyes, even her hair, they belonged to someone else. She explained that she didn't know
much, she still used her husband's name, but that for her it was as
though it were carved on a tombstone. I didn't care much for
that. She offered me tea. And while she busied herself in the
kitchen, asking me, raising her voice, if I took sugar, while I lis-
tened to the clatter of cups and saucers coming out of cupboards, I got up quietly from the chair and went into her
bedroom, Sugar, yes please, stepping into the shadow of her bed,
One or two?, One's fine, and I opened her closet. Her white
dress, the one she wore that December 31, her dress, I swear that
if I'd found it, I'd have asked her to wear it for me. But I didn't

find anything, not a trace, and I told myself that it really was her, then, Jeanne, still not giving herself away, not a trace.

I wouldn't have said that to Marin. I wouldn't have said anything to Marin except: I dropped in to see Jeanne and didn't enjoy it. That wasn't true. Actually, I did enjoy it, even seeing the dirty staircase and her shabby carpet, even the dreary light in her dining room, and the glaring absence of elegance, she was magnificent in her black skirt when she greeted me, with neither surprise nor joy nor unhappiness, but that unreadable look in her eyes, it was just like before. When she stared at me standing in her front hall, told me without the slightest show of emotion to come in, she didn't ask why or how I'd appeared there, or what I'd been doing for seven years, because for her, I'd always figured, the outside world is in parentheses. So what feeling could you express when the obvious is simply staring you in the face, personally I've never known, she makes my mind a blank, and I've often felt that, an inner emptiness, when I look at her. So when she poured out the tea in her old flowered cups, I decided it was time to go. I drank up my tea, thanked her, said I couldn't stay, just a thousand things to do, really so sorry. But she couldn't have cared less, she was still like that, even on the landing I wanted to say that I could stop by from time to time, I wanted to but I could already hear her answer, something like "If you want" or "Of course," something that committed only me, of course, if I wanted.

4

He lived at number 14. The name of the street I don't remember, but what counts for me now is that he doesn't live there anymore. At number 14, I wiped my feet for a long time on the doormat in the hall of the apartment building and I stared at the white cards on the mailboxes. I approached slowly, and gliding a fingertip across the letters, I read each name on the cards. His name, Luciano, was written larger than the others, in black letters. I took the edge of the card between thumb and index, pinched firmly, and tore the name from his mailbox. I remember whispering, Good-bye, Lucho.

Fifteen minutes after I rang his bell, I saw him come out, already breathless, suitcase in hand, with a scarf over part of his face, glancing up and down the sidewalk, no hesitation, to the right, he turned right and I fell in behind him, at a distance. Marin's voice was inside me repeating: There are two types of men, those who stay home waiting and those who run away. But it was obvious he'd be the second kind. And he turned around often, he'd stop in front of a shop window, using it as a mirror, but I was two hundred yards behind him, on the opposite sidewalk, so there was always something, a passerby, a streetlight, a car, to make me invisible. He didn't run, he was like a long-distance walker whose legs wobbled with the effort of moving swiftly. I never lost sight of him, even when he turned, because I knew the route he was taking, knew it down to the last inch.

He reached the train station in less than ten minutes. I could have waited for him there, I thought, waited on the platform the whole time, because it was just as I'd figured: the suitcase, the fear, the station. And I already suspected the destination. I watched him cross the concourse beneath the big clock and head for the ticket windows, where he got in line. He waited like everyone else, still looking all around him, then he spoke as little as possible with the clerk. When he turned to leave the counter, I saw that he was calmer, he felt reassured, as if by having his ticket already, or not being dead already, he'd sort of won his freedom. He checked his watch and saw that he had time, so he went off to the men's room. Me, across the concourse, I couldn't help myself, I followed him, into the rest room, and I spotted him, standing, from behind. I should have killed him then, but I didn't. I went over to the urinals, took the one right next to him, he didn't notice me, kept pissing, breathing hard. I made as if to piss as well, and next to him like that, half smiling, as he was zipping up, I said, These days, the train isn't any safer than a hot-air balloon.

And I saw his eyes bulge out of their sockets, his mouth suck up all the air in the room in one gulp. He didn't plan his next move, didn't keep his cool, didn't try to explain things, he took off like an animal without any second thought. He ran, I followed him, in no rush. Back in the concourse he looked up at the hands on the clock, then over at the departure times, people watched him gasping for breath, the clock, the platforms, next train at 2:17 P.M., it was two-something, 2:14. Next train, track 2, even the destination he probably didn't notice, he made a dash for it, so I did too, not as fast as he did. The train station wasn't noisy, only his footsteps rang out, mine behind his, and when he got his ticket punched in the silence of the concourse, when there was that sharp noise of the punch in the machine and the echo, he turned, looking frantically all around, and he felt the whole world was watching him. Don't worry, Lucho, you don't interest anyone here, not anyone except me. I almost hoped he would take it, that train, and that I would stay on the platform, and he would go away and never set foot in this city again. I thought that I must have changed, or gotten old, because seven years earlier, I thought, I'd have shot him down in the rest room. Afterward I'd have had a cognac in the station restaurant. In this game, when you start to let people get away, it's because you've already given up on it.

So I guess I hadn't given up on it. He got into the first car and kept watch at the window to see if I came down the platform. But he never did see me come down the platform, because I didn't arrive from the platform. I jumped down onto the empty tracks on the other side, track 1, and moved along the tracks, hunched over, hidden by the concrete, until I'd gotten past the first cars. When I climbed back onto the platform, I caught sight of his head through the window, still looking for me over by the concourse. And as the sound signal warned that the doors were closing, I hopped onto his train.

I could see him in my head, convinced now that the worst was behind him, I saw him settling into his compartment, hanging his jacket on the hook, collapsing into the soft seat, his back and buttocks sinking into the cushions, he would rub his hands together, smiling, and place his forearms on the rigid armrests, deliberately, like a calmly choreographed gesture. He must have smiled, yes, relaxed after his ordeal, calmed down, at peace, he must have smiled for a long while when the train began to move. His head as well, sinking slowly as well, deeply, into the leather headrest; drifting idly over the same landscape I saw, his gaze thought it had the scenery all to itself, the rapid departure from the city, the last stretches of sea rushing by with increasing speed, then the long green swath of an embankment, the long gray swath of the sky. Eyelids drooping closed, opening heavily again. Even his breathing must have returned to normal, abdomen gently collapsing, then gently expanding with that influx of air-conditioned air; installed in first class, he's soothed even by the colors, the garnet red, the blacks, anthracite.

Up on the platform between cars 5 and 6, no ticket, I pulled a door open with both hands, revolver hidden in my sleeve, I went along the corridor, checking every compartment, the doughy faces of businessmen, laptops on the pull-out tables, I pressed up against the corridor window to let a hefty guy go by, I looked behind me just from habit, then continued along the line of compartments, some of them empty, I lit a cigarette, inhaled eagerly, kept going, looking.

He probably hadn't dozed off to the muffled sound of the train. I imagined his head against the window, lips parted to receive the fresh air from the vent. But he must not have felt completely relaxed, because he was still afraid. There were surely a few gestures reflecting his satisfaction at being there: the hand he ran through his hair, the way he carefully brushed away a few flakes of dandruff clinging to his trousers, but the eyes, darting everywhere, seeking reassurance, and the sweat still beading on his skin—at times like that, you don't go to sleep.

Through the restaurant car, nonsmoking the waiter told me, but I didn't reply, I edged my way along the counter to the exit, car 3 I read at a glance on the liquid crystal display, I heaved open the sliding door, car 3, I grabbed the revolver, I'd find him.

I found him. Inside his compartment, beneath the reading lights in the ceiling shining their bright cones, the black window curtain was folded back next to him, his body awkwardly slumped in the seat. I stayed there a moment, silent, watching him through the glass panel of the door. He was perfectly still. At that moment he was definitely thinking of me, left far behind, alone on a platform. He turned of course, it's stronger than anything else, the presentiment of death, he turned and he shook his head, his eyes opening, he shook his head at seeing me, eyes wide open of course when he saw, not me looking at him but the flashy revolver I'd made a point of holding sideways in front of me, as if to show him it would soon be all over. We warned you a long time ago, Lucho: We never miss a one. I didn't smile. I opened the door. He would have liked to sink a bit deeper into his seat, not jump up or run, but disappear, melt away beneath the curtain, and his arms came up, and his mouth opened, but what movement would still be valid in another second, I thought for him. And I leveled the gun at him, the barrel perfectly aligned with his forehead. And without a flicker of emotion in my eyes, with him not even screaming, not even moaning, just choking, I fired. One bullet in the head, another in the heart.

Old business, Uncle would have said, settling old accounts. I got off at the next station and took a train going back in the other direction. I settled into first class, too, next to a window, and I saw the landscape stream by, the embankment, the first stretches of sea, the graffiti. I didn't think about him anymore, Lucho, or about his warm body slumped in a train. I didn't go back to my place. There are days like that, you take care of everything in your life, you settle all accounts.

5

So it was your turn, Marin.

I could have searched the whole world over for you. I would have devoted the rest of my life to it. But you must have learned as well, wandering from town to town, that one always encounters the same gaze, harbors the same suspicion about everyone, the same sense of being hunted forever, because for a long time now, Marin, your tired eyes have been seeing me in each passerby, and I've dreamed you so many times that you were bound to feel it. So then you tell yourself, of course, when that's the case, that you'd rather face up to the real threat, that even at the bottom of the sea, hiding under a rock, you'd have seen my face on every last fish in the ocean, and betrayal, for people like you, betrayal does not come naturally. So you made the right decision to come back home, to return to what you called a normal life and without any cops hassling you anymore, to come back home, Marin, and wait for me.

But when I rang his doorbell that day, when I held the button down with only the electric ringing echoing inside and bouncing off the bay window, I understood that he wasn't there, Marin, because even suspecting me, even seeing me in front of his gate, he would have let me in. He's the kind to hold out his arms in front of death, I said to myself, and I went inside anyway, through the door, because it was always open, because he used to say: Anybody steals from me in this city, he knows he's a dead man. And it was doubtless true, except that no one had ever tried. It was like those ideas that are in the air, wafting over the treetops, just part of the landscape.

Going into his place that afternoon, looking out the window at the sea, I did think there would be a dead man in the story, but it wouldn't be me. I searched, rummaged through papers, drawers, checked by the phone, and finally found in his memo book, under the binoculars, the note: 4:00, April 5, opera. A wall calendar still thumbtacked to that badly painted old wall said it was the fifth of April. It was 4:10.

I argued for a long time with the woman in the box office, I told her that I just wanted to see the second part, but that I was ready to pay full price. And I read on my ticket: matinee, adult admission, 120 F, 4:52. The name of the opera was also printed there, in Italian, because they were giving an Italian opera, with Italian singers onstage, and I slipped up to the first mezzanine, to a third-row box seat. The theater was Italian too, it's called à l'italienne when you can see everybody from the balcony. Me, in the dim light, I didn't watch much of the action. Of course I heard the singing going up into the rafters, of course I heard the emotion filling the air, the disturbance I created when I entered the box, when the light from the corridor shone in on people's heads. Even onstage they must have felt it, the disruption, the noise of the chair I moved, and the coughing that followed. In that kind of place, even with a thousand people, if one of them moves they all jump on him. If you think about it, I thought, a noisy chair or a gunshot, to them it's all the same. But I didn't see him, Marin, because it was dark everywhere, and onstage they seemed to be acting a sad part, so it was dark there too and you couldn't see any faces in the audience. Because for artists, I also thought, sadness goes well with darkness. If I went in for acting, I concluded, I would kill in broad daylight.

There was a big windup onstage and general applause. The lights came on, a giant chandelier came down from heaven, and everyone stood up. It was intermission. Taking advantage of the light, I went to the edge of the box and started searching. He was there, right across from me, in the first mezzanine, with some local big shots, waiting for the crowd to thin out, because him, he doesn't mix with crowds.

I can't say today if I wanted our eyes to meet at that moment or if I'd have preferred to surprise him in his seat, smile at him one last time and tip him into the orchestra, let him crash-land between two rows of seats and bleed all over the bloodred velvet. I can't say that, but I do know that I smiled at him anyway, leaning on the edge of the box, I smiled broadly to show him how happy I was to see him. Then he got up in a hurry and plunged into the thick of the crowd. He began to slalom among the jostled bodies, to thread his way through as best he could, you'd have thought he was swimming, with his arms held out in front of him to create a path, swimming and trying to keep his head above water. But you'll go under, Marin, you know you'll go under soon. And he kept weaving among the jackets, the well-tailored suits, half twisting to get around a couple, dodging down rows of seats, Sorry, excuse me, convinced I might pull out my piece any second and plug him at that distance, but you ought to know, Marin, that's not what I want.

He reached the door, so I figured it was time to stop smiling in his direction, as well as time to catch up with him on the steps out front. It was my turn to dart like a hare among the portly forms, the satisfied silhouettes, down the main staircase of the old theater, I glimpsed him ahead of me, he'd broken free of the crowd, of the press of perfumed flesh, while I now struggled to do the same, to advance, bumping into a back or a leg in my way, and people sputtered, shouted, yelled in outrage, dumbfounded by these two madmen, one chasing the other out into the cool, fresh air of an April afternoon.

He was looking behind him, running, racing down the long flight of steps, would have liked to protect himself, hide, take a hostage. But he knew I wasn't a judge or a cop, even a hostage wouldn't have kept me from shooting. He crossed the street without looking, cars jamming on the brakes, honking, me right behind him, and he vanished into the underground parking garage. I realized he was making for his Mercedes, I followed him down into the garage and ran into the front of the elevator, the closed doors of the elevator, and he was inside. I kicked the steel doors, a natural reaction, already thinking ahead, looking up at the red numbers over the elevator. He was on level 3.

I took the stairs to the left of the elevator and went down one level. He'd have to come by me to get up to the ground floor, and I'd wait for him. Lots of people were going up and down at that hour of the day, so I had to walk normally, a normal guy, in a normal little hurry. I pulled a set of keys from my pocket to pretend I was going to get a car, I jiggled them, then clutched them in my hand because of the jangling noise they made. I came out into the parking area, in the fluorescent lights, and looked for the spiral ramp that would bring him up from the depths. He was certain to appear soon, at the far end of the level, and his engine would be louder than expected, louder than the annoying sounds, the giant air vent, the humming of the fluorescent lights, the slamming doors, and the strange, hollow, metallic noises from who knows where. His tires would screech on the painted floor. He showed up, Marin, headlights blazing against the satiny black of the hood, at the wheel of his big German car. He saw me with my back to the wall dead ahead of him and he accelerated, from the far end of the aisle, he accelerated so much that I thought, for a second I thought, but when he saw my revolver aimed at the windshield, when he felt that I had his head in my sights, I swear, he turned the wheel right around, his hands were upside down on the rim, and his tires squealed like mad, the shrieking black rubber twisting under the weight of the chassis, he banged into a car, and another, the metal crumpling, smashing into the crappy concrete, he backed up and then headed for the exit.

I shot at the tires, the rear windshield, the trunk, some bullets hit home and glass went flying, but I saw him drive off without swerving. People had started screaming in front of the entrance and were scattering in all directions. I looked around quickly and saw a heavyset man getting into his car. I don't know if I bothered to apologize or what, but I stuck my gun under the guy's nose so he'd get the point. Sorry, chum, but when you've got a big car, someone just might swipe it. So I left him standing there and took off fast. I tossed my gun onto the passenger seat, to keep it handy, and went out into the dying light of the day.

I soon spotted the Mercedes on the highway. Streaking across town along the boulevards, running traffic lights in his fear, fleeing the city, Marin was an easy target. The zigzagging among the cars, the honking in his wake, and the roar of the engine gave him away even at a distance, it was like a drug rush for me. So maybe he'd rather have had three years in stir for speeding or DUI, maybe he'd have preferred a police ambush to my grim fury at his back. He was still far ahead and I could see his brake lights brighten as he came up on a curve. We reached the shore road. Him checking his rearview mirror, still dreaming of those absent words, that objects in it are closer than they appear, this time it must really have gotten to him. Fifteen years ago I'd told him, the day he wanted to install that mirror, I'd said it was a bad move, those words that fascinated him were a bad warning, I'd said, you shouldn't clutter up your life with heavy stuff. But Marin, his life, he crammed it absolutely full. And now he was almost smothered in his old Mercedes, on that winding road above the cliffs, braking for each curve, tires edging into the dirt and screeching on the asphalt, like two forces in perpetual contradiction, Marin's willpower and the laws of physics on the road, the whole car fishtailing on the rear wheels, then barreling on. I kept closing the distance on him, wound up right on his tail, breathing down his neck. Some situations are like that, you know who's in charge, and nothing can change that. I sped up, tapped his bumper on the straightaway, softly at first, then rammed it harder, and blasted the horn, and I was gritting my teeth like crazy, and glaring at him like crazy. The chase went on for miles. He kept swerving, the cylinders coughing as they caught their breath, the turns getting sharper, I pulled up on his right, with just enough room to skirt the ditch along the road, and wrenched the wheel, slamming my left front fender into his door, once, twice, the dull, muffled sound of the steel, and he veered off to the left, toward the cliff, toward the drop, the last few feet of earth before the plunge, he'd lost control, the road, the shoulder, a cloud of dust went up and for a second he disappeared in that spray of dirt and pebbles, his wheels lost traction in the loose soil, as if in helpless fury, but he came out of it, whipped the wheel around, still skidding forward, and then one wheel gripped the asphalt, and another, hurtling on, fleeing the void, then he was back on the road, our two cars side by side, two dragsters going full out, and I saw him looking at me, his fixed smile, light from somewhere shining on his face, his hands clearly visible on the wheel, he was baring his teeth at me, the constant grinding noise of metal crumpling, we were still neck and neck, scraping the paint from the doors, the boom of battered steel, I lowered my window, grabbed the revolver from the passenger seat, one hand on the wheel, the other aiming at his window, I pulled the trigger and shattered the glass. The engine noise drowned out even the gunshots but I'd missed him, he straightened up and now it was his turn to fire at me, and I had time to imagine the spark, the flame darting from the muzzle of the gun, but I'd already ducked and then I braked hard and soon there was nothing left to see but a plume of exhaust, nothing to hear but a last growl from the engine as he vanished around the curves.

You don't beat Marin like that, even when he's down, even when he's already done for and heading for disaster. Even suicidal he can still win. I wiped the sweat and dirt from my face with a handkerchief, downshifted, went flat out, and it was like an airplane taking off, that car, it just exploded. I thought for a moment it was American, a Corvette or something like that, but I know zip about cars. All I know is, Marin has had the same Mercedes for fifteen years, and it's no slouch either—he used to say it spat fire and ate up the road. Well, Marin, now you'll see which car can spit the farthest. Whenever I changed gears the needles on the dashboard seemed to whirl completely around three times, but he'd raced on out of sight. I figured I'd catch up with him fast in the turns ahead, along the coast.

And in fact when I saw him I was closing fast, but he was coming straight at me, his radiator grille like a baleen whale sucking in air, our two cars bearing down on each other at top speed, the both of us holding our revolvers up by the wheel, like two horsemen, two duelists trying to run each other through with swords, windows open, ready to fire in passing, two, three bullets on either side shattering the windshields, I got him in the arm, I thought I'd gotten him in the arm, because of the way he swerved immediately afterward, but he straightened out immediately too, I'd only hit the seat and rattled him.

We should have settled things right then, pulled our battered heaps over and slugged it out, but he'd turned the car around for more, more punishment for him and me. And at that point I could have driven away, in other words, abandoned the battlefield, leaving only the lingering threat of a return engagement. I could have. But what pushes us to grip the leather of the steering wheel, to keep our arms rigid and our spines firmly set against the seat back—no one can say what part of ourselves speaks in that moment, and makes us go on.

The road still twisted and turned above the drop. There were islands on the horizon, visible against the cloudless sky, like black bumps in the calm blue sea and the limpid late-afternoon light. I flipped down the sun visor and saw, looming ahead of us, still far in the distance, the ruins of an abbey we'd often joked about when we drove past—Andrei especially, he used to say the stones were so decrepit they were part of the "family." Set on the edge of the cliff near the old abbey out on the point was a lighthouse, warning of treacherous rocks lurking just below the surface. The road kept getting more tortuous, more dangerous. Our tires had taken a beating and were screaming at each turn, disturbing the silence of the ruins and the grass that had grown up all around them, around the flagstones, and the stone columns we could see now from the road, winding by them, driving past them, it was like a straight line plunging into the sea, breaking off there, at the end of the stones, at the foot of the white lighthouse, in the ninety-foot drop off the bluff, which because of the turn at the end you couldn't see, could only guess at, only suppose was there, but which was hidden by the sun in your face until you were right on top of it. The tired stones measured off the distance and I thought, shooting straight for the sea, I thought, I'm not going to take that turn. So instead of braking sharply as I should have, instead of hugging the road, I kept hurtling on, Marin behind me letting in the clutch, and it just flashed across my mind—the car sailing over, belly flopping into the water, like slamming into a concrete wall, the rocks right at the surface, the door jammed under the cold water—I thought, I'll try it, I'll forget about the turn and jump out before the drop. Marin was following and couldn't see anything of the precipice ahead, so close, he would go over the edge in his Mercedes without enough time to bail out. I sped up, checked to see he was right on my tail, then more speed, third, fourth, the tachometer went into the red, the sea dead ahead, 70, 80, I floored it, a last glance in the rearview mirror, the sea still dead ahead and filling the horizon, 90, I undid the belt, one hand on the door, a last pump of the accelerator, the door, the wheel held steady not swerving an inch, the door, the car on the edge of the cliff, the door handle, and with a great heave of my shoulder I dove out the side. I went out headfirst, rolled, hit hard again and again, the car driving on into the sunset, out to the sea, over the rocks, dropping suddenly in the abrupt silence of the engine, and Marin coming on behind, yelling, I saw his wide-open mouth and sun-dazzled eyes, following me, my car, blind to the abyss staring him in the face or not yet realizing that my car was already underwater, dead ahead, and I screamed, Jump, Marin, jump! I screamed again and saw a form fly out at the last instant, tumbling across the stubby grass, Marin, with barely enough time to see the Mercedes take off. I'd thought he wouldn't leave it, his Mercedes, as if he'd become part of it, fossilized forever in its metal matrix, and would crash with it into the brutal sea. That wasn't what I wanted.

The Mercedes, already rusting beneath the waves, where from now on only sardines would peek at themselves in the rearview mirror.

He was ten yards from me. I stood up before he did, gripping my revolver. I could have fired. I stretched out my arms and aimed at him, but he was still dazed and crumpled on the ground, I'd have emptied the clip into his back but I couldn't, because that wasn't what bound us together, not a bullet in the back. My precise thought was: That's not what keeps us under the same sky. So I ran as best I could to the ruins, body bruised and knees aching, I limped, more like it, and hid behind the first stone, out of breath.

6

The wind had died down, as if wanting to leave us alone, as if even the sky wanted us to settle our accounts without it, the dry air barely touching our faces. We could no longer see each other. I kept my finger right on the trigger and I'm sure at that moment he was doing the same, behind a column, revolver held head high, each of us waiting for the other to show himself. There were the stones and grass open to the sky in the ruins, the towering lighthouse, the sun setting over the sea and the possible betrayal—him or me or both of us—the possible betrayal of a blundering shadow. And I cracked first, I felt first the need he'd have felt a second later to move. I ran from one pillar to another, a headlong dash, fifteen endless feet, and in fact he fired, he came out from behind a column too, he fired, but he missed me. I laughed loudly, and he heard the echoing stones join in. But his only answer was the revolver he reloaded, the clatter of the clip he snapped in at that very moment, nervously, I suppose, each of us wanting to get the other's life or death over with, fast.

I don't know what happened then, since the shots seemed to go off simultaneously, both of us first risking our arms from behind the walls, then darting completely out in the open, arms extended shooting, we ran, we hid, jumping, ducking, still firing, emptying our clips, the bullets ricocheting, you'd have thought we'd choreographed our performance to avoid ever meeting up, or ever taking a bullet fired off too soon, as if we had to carry out the rites due such a death, the tribal dance, the movements performed by our bodies, we let fly with more bullets, and did some more running around, grabbing onto stone pillars as if they were dance partners we hated to leave, breathless, cringing, strung out from focusing every fiber of our being on the other guy.

And he's the one who drew first blood. A bullet in the leg. I screamed, kept moving, clutching my thigh and feeling the burning in my thigh, the hot brass in my thigh, the scream that brought me to my knees, and I lay down on the gravel, bit my lip hard and crawled over behind a low wall. The stones, that day, we loved every last one of them. I held in my breath and my blood, I saw only his legs and the shadow his gun cast, which grew longer with my pain. I tied my handkerchief around my thigh, and I had the feeling, he was so close, Marin, I knew he would die at my hands.

I hadn't let go of my piece the whole time, there were three bullets left, I counted, and I murmured: Tomorrow you'll be at peace with yourself. I saw it all in a flash, his shattered face on the ground, the cigars he smoked, the bottle of cognac, I saw the bullet I'd fire in cold blood into his skull, I saw Jeanne and the money, all the money, forever, I saw. Several times I felt our shadows melting together, our breaths mingling in the air, so near, and the bullets whistling past our ears. I felt how simple it was to obliterate life in a burst of gunfire. Then he hid too, and everything grew quiet again. I slipped into the damp grass; he was protected where he was by granite, but I was more invisible because of the high grass in that area. I didn't see him, I felt him, I felt the sunlight seeking out his weapon, the stone contracting at the touch of his breath. I had three bullets left. I heard the sharp sound of the clip across from me but I'd already understood—as far as ammunition was concerned, I hadn't a chance. I thought, I'll get my chance talking to him, I'll speak to him, we'll talk, and meanwhile I'll get closer, I'm talking, and I take him by surprise. Listen, I said, okay, you've got the advantage from now on, okay, you can finish me off now, but you're a stand-up guy, Marin, you're a stand-up guy, I said, you know what a debt means. And I kept sneaking up on him, slowly, through the grass, crouching under the prickly evergreen shrubs, wriggling through the thistles, the wild plants. Listen to me, Marin, you cough up a million, you pay your debt in cash, and you come out of it on top, you come out of it bigger than ever, you've won against me and against yourself. And I forgot my pain, getting closer, another few yards. And then he started talking, he told me we'd never be quits, I must know that, it wasn't what I was after, we'd never be quits just through money. And I finished crawling toward him, still listening to him, keeping close to the granite block he was using as a shield, I said, We'll be quits soon enough, and I stood up behind him. Yes, Marin, we'll be quits soon enough.

Silence, a fraction of an instant without anything, not a

word or gesture, because it had been a long, long time since we'd seen each other up so close. I punched him in the jaw, and grabbed him by the neck, we were worn-out, both of us disheveled, gasping, drenched in sweat, he hit me back, in the belly, the head, we were like fighters in an arena, without weapons, yet certain it was to the death. Because we'll have respected each other right to the end, Marin and I, from friendship, we'd have said, if we'd taken time out to think about it, like kids in a school playground, from friendship. Like the way we were always aware of each other's presence, a reflection of our mutual awe and respect, like the way bloodshot eyes grow wide with wonder. We caught our breath for a moment, just a moment, but he took off running among the walls weathered by centuries, winds, salt air, he was exhausted, and so was I. I looked up at the white lighthouse, saw him slip inside the door, seeking refuge, and I hesitated, but I headed for the lighthouse, because I had to. In the staircase he was like a ghost in a whirlwind, he climbed, up the two hundred and twenty-three steps tallied in big letters at the entrance, and I went up, I went up after him, in a corkscrew, I clung to the rail, we were panting like animals.

The two of us, all the way up, out on the circular platform, each wondering what the hell we were doing there, at the top of a lighthouse. He was done in. I went over to him, empty-handed, no weapon, no raised fist. He held up one hand as if in supplication, as if wanting to say one last thing, in one last breath, he was trying to find the air to say something, a tremor ran through his body, a slight smile floated to his lips and with a last sigh he said, It was . . . the absolute . . . perfection . . . of . . . crime. And he smiled through the blood in his mouth. I looked up, out to sea. The light had come to a halt for us, with the orange disk of the sun vanishing below the horizon and the sea sparkling with tiny rainbows through the tears in my eyes. I headed for the stairs again, calmly, and I didn't look back.